Murkier than

Lee Koss

ISBN: 9798754386099

Any references to historical events, real people, or real places are used fictitiously. Names, characters, and places are products of the author's imagination.

Front cover image by Lee Koss

First printing edition 2021

leekossbooks@gmail.com

About the author

Lee Koss, *nom de plume*, was born and raised on Merseyside. Before his writing career, he worked in marketing and communications.

Murkier than the Mersey is the author's first novel set in the city of Liverpool.

PART ONE
FRIDAY NOVEMBER 13 TO MONDAY NOVEMBER 16, 2020

One

Friday afternoon, November 13, 2020

'Welcome to Liverpool ladies and gentlemen! No need to have your masks on outside. Take a deep breath and suck in that beautiful local air wafting down from the Liver Building over there and off the emerald and blue colours of the River Mersey. And if you're looking for immunity against COVID, go no further - a glass of uniquely refreshing Mersey River water will do the trick.

Let me introduce myself. My name's Steve Whittley, Liverpool's leading tour guide. Liverpool. Capital of pop, from the Beatles to Frankie goes to Hollywood and beyond. We also call the place Ireland's second city, because of the hundreds of thousands of Irish who fled the potato famine in 1840, with many settling here, including some of my ancestors. This city is also Covid capital of the country as we speak.

Thanks again for coming here in person. We'll be outdoors for the duration of this tour to reduce the risk of contagion. At least we're still allowed to host small, socially distanced groups such as ours here today. And now you're here I'm sure you'll agree that Zoom just doesn't do it. Like watching the magnificent Reds behind closed doors, with no Kop to give you those goose pimples. Yes, folks, you guessed correctly. I support the world's greatest football team, Liverpool FC where you'll never walk alone!

When I was a kid in the seventies this whole area was a bunch of rubble, not yet cleaned up from those second world war bombs which destroyed a lot of the old port. They also knocked out the appalling slums down here that housed the unwashed, like my grandad Bill. A blessing in disguise.

Our two big cathedrals are now finished. Paddy's wigwam, the Catholic one, took twenty years to build and already needs a re-fit. I just love that name, don't you? And the imposing, neo-gothic Anglican one looking down on us from over there took over seventy years to finish. The largest cathedral in the country, with the biggest organ as well. Grim on the outside, awesome on the inside. Survived the blitz, unlike the bombed-out church at the end of Bold Street that we'll visit later.

Liverpool's a poor city and it's taken over seventy years to rebuild since the war. But now things are looking up, especially for our city councillors' wallets, I'm told. We've got Liverpool One, one of the UK's leading shopping centres. Thank you Dukey, the late Duke of Westminster for financing that. And look at all that residential housing development since then over there. The Ropewalks, the Baltic Triangle, the Knowledge Quarter. I won't say any more about this. But keep your eyes glued to the local papers for updates. Some serious wheeler dealing going on and it's getting murkier by the day. Murkier than the river Mersey if you ask me.

Madam, you have a question?'

'Who owns all these swanky new residential properties?'

'Now that's a loaded question Ms.?'

'Ma, Julie Ma.'

'Most of this new stuff was built by the Sharkey Group. Luke Sharkey is one of the city's richest men. Local lad. He's to Liverpool what Donald Trump was to New York before becoming President. The apartments are now owned by wealthy people from down south and abroad. It's a buy-to-let scheme I'm told, but I don't have all the details. You should do an online search with the keywords *Sanjay Singh*, *Liverpool Post,* and *Luke Sharkey*. That will tell you all you need to know about this funny business, Ms. Ma.'

'Thanks. Was just curious.'

'OK. Let's keep moving. The one and only Liver Building is up next.'

Two

Friday evening, November 13, 2020,
Liverpool Royal Hospital, Accident and Emergency
Department

Sanjay Singh's journey to England was very different from most British Sikhs. He was the only child of Charan and Seema Singh, who'd arrived in the city directly from India when Sanjay was ten years old. In the late eighties his dad Charan Singh, a top finance executive, had been headhunted to take over the role of Chief Financial Officer at the national HQ of GiroPostBank, based in the city. The main focus of the bank for the past fifty years had been cheque-clearing. By the turn of the century, Charan had worked himself out of a job, but the redundancy package was top notch and he and Seema had moved back to India for the good life. Sanjay had stayed in Liverpool where the *Liverpool Post* had hired him as a rookie journalist straight out of university.

That evening Sanjay was on his weekly scouting visit to the old Liverpool Royal Hospital. Accident and Emergency department, that's where the action was. Stories there, galore. Good old morbid stuff, the kind that made his readers feel better.

The new hospital, just around the corner from the old, was finished but had been vacant for the past three years. What a farce! The country's National Health Service spending all that money heating and lighting the place, but with no patients. What a waste of taxpayers' money.

Ever since Carroll Inc., the building contractors, went bankrupt four years ago, nobody seemed to care. Even the city's Mayor, Don Ferguson, seemed to have thrown in the towel.

Sanjay had already penned some pieces about this stupidity in the *Post*, but this time was different. With Covid hitting Liverpool hard, he wanted a story to kick dirt with those central government toffs down south, hopelessly out of touch with his hometown.

What could that story be? No room at the inn? Doctors playing God during this third Covid wave? Unused ventilators in an unopened new hospital? There must be an angle somewhere. Just got to find the hook.

Downstairs in the coffee area of the Victorian hospital Sanjay tilted the vending machine to get the *KitKat* bar to fall. Taking off his Everton Football Club branded facemask, he devoured the wafers in five bites. He'd not eaten, having rushed to the hospital on the news from his hospital insider source that Luke Sharkey, that young, dynamic, and totally bent Liverpool Property Tycoon, was on a life support ventilator with Covid, they said.

The virus has already picked off a few younger victims in the city, all with pre-existing conditions. Given his asthma condition, Luke Sharkey was considered vulnerable. Still, at not yet forty years old, it did seem a little premature and even sad, though Sanjay wondered if anyone could possibly feel one ounce of sympathy for such a ruthless and unscrupulous crook.

Just yesterday he'd re-read one of the many articles he'd penned for the *Post* about Sharkey, the one about his arrest by the city's fraud police, along with the Liverpool City Council Regeneration Officer, Mickey Cavandish. They'd found hundreds of thousands of pounds in used notes in Sharkey's penthouse flat. But no charges were levelled against either man by the police. And Sharkey had since had the gall to successfully sue the police for unlawful entry into his flat, forcing the police to suspend DI Steve Whittley, the detective leading the raid.

People like Luke Sharkey were manna from heaven for crime reporters like Sanjay. Sharkey always managed his businesses close to the wire. He mastered the fine line between legality and illegality, and if people were prepared to be purchased, then so be it! There were many more stories in the Sharkey property saga for Sanjay to craft and weave. And maybe he'd get some syndicated stuff in some national red tops, both on and offline. His social media influencer status was right up there. He'd done everything right. But what counted most was he loved his job. And was very good at it. The leading crime editor in a high-crime city. But now a leading *ink-spiration source*, as he liked to call Sharkey, was dying of Covid. Not fair, dammit.

Sipping his instant vending machine coffee, Sanjay's attention moved to a pretty woman across the hall talking into her mobile with intensity. Was that a Spanish accent? Latin American, probably. She seemed to be talking hurriedly in a tone that denoted urgency. Putting his prescription glasses back on he recognised her. It was Lania. Lania

Reyes, or Lania Sharkey as she was now called following her recent marriage to Luke Sharkey, Liverpool's richest man, now on life support in an emergency ward nearby.

No prizes for guessing why she was here, poor woman. She must be devastated.

Three

Friday evening, November 13, 2020, Liverpool Royal Hospital

'You know Mary,' Joe Sharkey said to his sister, 'I'm so sorry. I don't think he's going to make it. So sad. Such a great kiddo. Done so well for himself. Re-building our city centre almost single-handed. And if only the management of Everton Football Club had accepted his takeover bid. Then he'd have realised his greatest ambition. Owning the club's even better than playing for it. Bloody asthma. Such a great young footballing talent he was. Could've been the new Howard Kendall. I'm sorry, sis, I'm so sorry.

And you've been such a great Mum. Asshole for a father though, poor lad. At least the prick left before he beat you and the kid to pulp.

I know sis. I know that you can't face seeing him die. Your only kid. I understand. I'll be with him until the end. Maybe he'll make it. Docs don't sound hopeful though. I'm praying with him, Mary. Stay strong sis. Stay strong.'

As Joe Sharkey was on the phone with his sister, Luke's mother, Lania Sharkey, Luke's wife, was speaking to a very close friend.

'Hi Diane, my phone's almost dead. Got to get back to the ward now. Or as close as they'll allow me to it. His Uncle Joe's there as well. But his Mum can't face it. Went home a few hours ago. Can't say I blame her. Poor Mary.

Yes, I did get the urine sample. It's in his clothes bag. I'll pass by your flat with it later. Still trying to figure out why you want that?

Yes, I love you too. But he's my husband. He helped me. He saved me. I'd still be in that hole without him, you know that my love. No, we never had that big wedding he promised, I know. But he promised me, and you never know. I've always lived in hope Diane, I believe in God and He will provide for me now.

What Diane? Cremation? Burning him? How can I talk to his Mum about that? He's not even dead yet. The family tradition is burial. Why cremation?

No, I won't forget what an asshole he could be sometimes. Including to me. But now he's dying Diane. So let's just give him some respect. And then it will be our time together, for each other.

Yes, he signed that life insurance policy three months ago, Diane. Didn't I tell you that already?

I have to stay here. I'll call you if it changes. Besos. T'amo....

Diane, are you still there? The doctor's just come out. He's dead. Oh my God. Luke's dead. What have you done Diane?'

From over by the vending machine, Sanjay Singh watched and listened.

Nestled cosily on her sofa in her apartment in Walker Square in the Ropewalks area of Liverpool city centre, Diane ended the call with Lania. She felt no remorse at all.

Just a few minutes later she answered another incoming call.

'Julie Ma? The answer is Yes.'

The call lasted less than five seconds and Diane hung up again.

Four

Later that same evening

It was a surprisingly warm and calm mid-autumn evening, rare in Liverpool, a city known more for its high-velocity wind and horizontal rain. Before leaving the hospital for home, Sanjay took a walk down by the river. He needed some air to clean out the stuffy, chlorinated smells of the place clinging to his clothes. Crossing the road just past the bus station, he entered the majestic Albert Dock, named after Prince Albert, Queen Victoria's husband.

It was built around an area that harboured a darker past of slave trading, a traffic that financed many of the finer buildings and homes in the centre built in the eighteenth century. The talk was now of changing the names of the city streets that carried the reminders of those traders of yesteryear. Not before time, thought Sanjay.

The red-brick UNESCO world heritage structure reflected eerily in the glass-still water with memories of Victorian sailors, dockers and tradesmen loading and unloading merchandise to and from the colonies of the British empire and the new world. A hustle and bustle of former jingoistic glory. An age of sail, rope, masts, and adventure to the far-flung extremities of a bygone world when Britannia ruled the waves. A time that many in the country were now looking back to with a strange nostalgic sense of pride and achievement. Weird.

In 2016 a majority in the nation had voted to leave the European Union to create a new Global Britain, as they called it. But Sanjay knew better and had voted to remain, worried about the inevitable lowering of social and environmental standards. His city, Liverpool, had also voted to remain in Europe. Most Liverpudlians trusted their central government rulers in London even less than the overpaid Eurocrats in Brussels. The city's mayor had funded lobbyists in Brussels who helped Liverpool benefit massively from European funds for depressed regions, with the town being nominated the European City of Culture back in 2008. Would the mandarins in London have ever agreed to that level of funding? For Liverpool? For scumbag, stealing scousers? No way, thought Sanjay as he reflected on his hometown.

In normal times the Albert Dock would be flooded with visitors from all over the world. There were still some small, socially distanced tourist parties around, but not many. Pre-Covid, the Albert Dock had become one of the UK's top attractions, the Liverpool Arena and the Tate Gallery. But Covid had cleared the decks and Sanjay had the walkways to himself, with a few lone joggers and cyclists.

He headed up to the Liver Building, another of the city's famous landmarks, a large Victorian building with two strange-looking birds attached by wire and mounted on small steeple-like structures over the clocks, the Liver Birds. Bella and Bertie.

From there he glanced further up the river to Bramley Dock. In just a few short years from now, this derelict blast from the past would be transformed into England's best football stadium for the country's greatest football team, the Toffees, Everton FC. *Come On You Blues!* rang out inside his head.

Sanjay then headed eastwards, inland. He preferred to live in the city centre, close to the Merseyside Police HQ from where his insiders fed him regular bites. On foot from his place, he could also make it to the hospital in less than fifteen minutes, where he'd mingle outside with the cigarette-smoking nurses alongside the ambulance-chasing lawyers. They were always onto something and provided a valuable source when other stories dried up.

Sanjay lived in a new build, one-bedroom apartment in Tradewinds Square, next to Chinatown. The Liverpool property tycoon, and now dead Luke Sharkey, had offered him a knock-down price on an apartment he'd built in Walker Square in the nearby Ropewalks neighbourhood. He'd been tempted. A twenty-thousand discount would have given Sanjay an additional bedroom, and with all his paper junk he definitely needed the space. But deep down he knew that Luke Sharkey would never do such a favour out of the goodness of his heart. No free lunch with him, that's for sure. In fact, *no free lunch* was one of the first lessons he'd learned as a journalist.

His place still housed some bargain-basement student furniture that the previous tenant, a post-doc from The Gambia working at the Liverpool School of Tropical Medicine, had left there. Sanjay's study table in the bedroom was overflowing with clippings, dailies, weeklies, and a pile of photocopies, most of them involving Luke Sharkey and his property development company, the Sharkey Group. On the big trunk case which doubled up as a table in front of the ceiling-to-floor window were pictures of his Mum and Dad on their wedding day in India, and of a selection of the cricket teams he'd played in since his schooldays.

Pouring himself his favourite *Aberlour* single-malt Scotch, he called his old schoolmate, Steve Whittley, who was also his best friend.

'Hi there, no balls, it's me, Sanj. What's up.'

No balls was Sanjay's nickname for Steve. They'd been friends since the age of eleven when they'd started together at the Bluecoat School, one of the city's more prestigious schools, though not fee-paying like that toff school Merchant Taylors.

They were both avid cricketers and they still played the game in the same team on summer Sundays, for the third eleven at Liverpool Cricket Club.

'Have you heard the news?' Sanjay said. 'Luke Sharkey's dead, Steve, dead.'

'Sharkey? That narcissistic sociopath who stitched me up. Hallelujah! Dead? From what? Accident? Someone eventually had the good sense to throw him under a bus?'

'Well, that's the rub, Steve. He died with Covid, apparently, earlier this evening in the A&E. I was there, sniffing around, and overheard some conversations. Something didn't seem right. A gut feeling, Steve. Could be murder.'

'Murder? Didn't realise you could deliberately and knowingly murder someone with Covid? Difficult to do, let alone prove in court. You persuaded me to search Luke Sharkey's house and that got me suspended, didn't it? So, you can count me out if you're looking for help, mate.'

'Let me explain.'

'Look, Sanj, if you're looking for a murder story for the *Post*, don't get me involved. I've got to lie low at present. You know how I feel about Luke Sharkey. I did the right thing, followed my boss's orders to put the crook away, where he belongs, then *I'm* the one who gets suspended! It's all wrong.'

'I know Steve, and we're working to get your suspension lifted. And this is the thing: If we can prove that Sharkey's been murdered, then DCI McCartney will re-instate you, I'm sure of it.'

'You think so?'

'I know so.'

'And you'll get your story as well, of course.'

'I will. A win-win situation. This is a big story for me, Steve. A story for a whole weekend edition, maybe more. And it could help you get your badge back. We need to work together. Nobody has a better copper's nose than you, Steve. In or out mate? And don't say *no ball*.'

'*No ball*, Sanj.'

'I'm not taking no for an answer. I need you to dig around. I listened in on Sharkey's wife's telephone conversation with a friend as her husband was dying. She was talking with someone called Diane. Struck me as strange. Weird conversation. They seemed close, very close.'

'Lania Sharkey? That dolled-up young Venezuelan hooker? Sharkey's trophy wife?'

'She wasn't a hooker Steve, you know that. You read my articles. She's been used and abused throughout her short life. Used by the escort bar that employed her in Panama. Used by her Venezuelan family that was happy to live off the money she sent home. Used by Luke Sharkey in more ways than one. And now I think she's being used again, by Diane, whoever she is.'

'If you say so.'

'I do. And I need your crime-sniffer instinct on this one. Why would her friend Diane want a urine sample? I heard it clearly Steve, a urine sample. Doesn't that strike you as suspicious?'

'Suspicious, or not, I've got to pick my fights carefully these days. Luke Sharkey and his city council cronies? Together they've created a nasty little mafia group, taking this city in the wrong direction. Now I'm suspended, I really don't need any more hassle from them. No more heroics for me,' Steve said, wanting to finish the conversation.

'My God! Guess who just texted me, Steve? Lania Sharkey. Says she wants to speak to me about an obituary for her husband in the *Post* tomorrow. That's quick! Could it have been pre-prepared, do you think? Will get back to you soon pal. Meantime, try to find your balls, Steve. They're out there somewhere.'

Five

Liverpool Post, Saturday, November 14, 2020.

Tribute to our Founder, Chairman, and CEO, Mr. Luke Sharkey

This page has been paid for by the Sharkey Group, the North West's leading high-class residential housing development company.

It is with utmost sadness and with a heavy heart that the Sharkey Group announces the untimely and premature passing of its cherished Founder, Chairman, and CEO, Mr. Luke Sharkey on Friday, November 13, 2020. Mr. Sharkey, who suffered from chronic asthma, died with Covid at just 39 years old. In those years he achieved more than most men double his age.

Having grown up on the terraced streets of Wavertree in the city of Liverpool, he went from a promising Everton Football Club Academy player to property magnate at the top of a £1bn development empire.

At the time of his death, Luke Sharkey was promoting a host of major residential developments in Liverpool, including the riverside Paradise Towers project, Liverpool's tallest building to date. Sharkey's business life began after he was told he would not be able to continue at the Everton FC Academy, his boyhood football club, at 15 years of age. The Academy let him go when he was diagnosed with asthma, which the club thought would hold him back from true greatness. That was to come elsewhere. Leaving the Academy was a turning point for Mr. Sharkey. 'You either crumble or you pick yourself up, dust yourself down and crack on. I cracked on', said the man with the typical grit and courage that we at the Sharkey Group know and admire so well.

Sharkey was forever grateful to his mother, Mary, who brought him up after his abusive father left, saying that his Mum was the 'single biggest factor' behind his success, and that 'she fought tooth and nail to ensure that I focused on what was right. She gave me the values that have carried me through my career. I can't credit her enough.'

After the Academy failure, Sharkey opted for an apprenticeship at sewage pipe and wire maker M.E. Pimms. 'In simple terms, we designed the pipes and wires that run through buildings and make them work and I found my niche. The company was a great employer and put me through an Ordinary National

Certificate then my Higher National Certificate. Yes, I was naturally gifted at what I did, but always wanted more.' Sharkey said that during his apprenticeship, he 'paid attention, asked questions outside his remit and stuck his nose into areas of the business that only the high-potential would do'.

He then made his first leap, creating companies to buy city-centre freeholds. 'It was fun and I learned a lot about running companies and all the aggro that goes with that. I saw a chance to move into property development and grabbed it with both hands.' With internet firms, games designers, and architects moving in, Sharkey sensed the development potential and had the vision to invest in freeholds in the blighted Baltic Triangle and Ropewalks areas of the city.

He sold out his first Sharkey Group residential development, the Essential Luxuries on Jamaica Street, within three months to overseas investors. Promoting his developments to foreigners under a scheme called 'Future Financing' was a model that Sharkey used many times over his all too short career at the apex of Liverpool's city regeneration and renovation. From that first completed scheme in 2013, Sharkey amassed a development pipeline of more than a billion pounds sterling.

As well as the Liverpool projects that included Mayfair Mall, Harrison Wheat Mill and Walker Square in the Ropewalks, he was always working on the next, more ambitious development. A true visionary, Sharkey put his success down to 'working with people who have the skills and experience you lack. The best entrepreneurs, like me, surround themselves with people who are even better than them in every sphere. We only hire HPs – high potentials, in common parlance. This is why I have the best project managers, engineers, architects, and more on tap. We debate and argue the toss continuously, but it drives us towards the highest levels of performance. And with so many plates spinning, that's vital.'

Throughout his all-too-short life, Sharkey remained true to his beloved hometown. 'Almost all my supply chain is from Liverpool and I'm intensely proud of that. Every development we do delivers work for local trades and keeps more of our investment in the city. I create jobs for the working classes, humble people like me who've known hard times and want to get ahead through the toil of their own efforts,' Sharkey said in a recent interview in the Liverpool Post.

In the same article, Sharkey went on to reiterate his unwavering support for the business-friendly policy of the City Council. 'Liverpool wants jobs, and the council is proactive in encouraging investment, which is great. The planners demand quality and keep my design team on their toes and that's good too as everyone benefits from better architecture. Both our Mayor, Don Ferguson, and Mickey Cavandish, the

City Council Regeneration Officer, have been truly inspiring. Without them, none of this could have happened.'

Perhaps the greatest disappointment for Mr. Sharkey was the rejection by Everton FC, his boyhood football club of his takeover offer, valued at £700 million. Sadly, and almost certainly to their detriment, the club's management did not share the acute vision of the late Luke Sharkey.

Due to Covid restrictions, only a small number of family and friends will be permitted to attend the cremation, scheduled for Monday, 16th November.

We send our deepest condolences to his mother, Mrs. Mary Sharkey, his uncle, Mr. Joe Sharkey, and his widow, Mrs. Lania Sharkey.

Six

Sunday evening, November 15, 2020
Sanjay Singh's flat

Just after eight o'clock in the evening, Sanjay opened the door of his apartment to his old mate Steve Whittley, Detective Inspector Steve Whittley. To be precise, *suspended* Detective Inspector Steve Whittley.

Steve took his place on the sofa in front of the small balcony looking straight into the apartment on the other side of the street.

'Mind if I close the blinds, Sanj? I'm not supposed to be here unless you've put me in your Covid bubble.'

'*No Balls*, you'll always be part of my bubble, Covid or no Covid.'

On the sidewall, Steve spotted a couple of framed photos from their school cricket eleven hanging there, proudly. Have I really changed that much, thought Steve? Sanjay looked just the same. He'd hardly aged at all. Jealous? No.

They'd both had very successful careers so far, Steve in the force and Sanjay at the *Liverpool Post*. Could it be that police work had aged him more quickly? They should offer a Botox allowance these days to middle-aged coppers, men and women alike.

'Hey, Sanj. Got a present for you.'

Steve reached into his pocket and brought out a Liverpool Football Club Covid face mask.

'It's all the rage. This red LFC face mask has the best defensive record in the country, stopping all germs penetrating from inside or outside the goalmouth. It's a must-have for all discerning Covid fans.'

'Thanks, Steve. But I beat you to it.'

Sanjay immediately put on his own Everton FC face mask. Oh, those Toffees, such losers, thought Steve.

'No sign of a Covid vaccination yet, pal. We're going to have to get used to this crap. It's going to be a long haul, mate. What are we going to do about this Luke Sharkey business? Guess that's why I'm breaking the law to be here at your urgent request?'

Sanjay explained to Steve how he'd been writing stories about Luke Sharkey for many years and how he'd still got no closer to the man behind the face. Sharkey was an enigma. Was he Liverpool's Robin

19

Hood? Or, more likely, one of the most unscrupulous property developers the city had known since its glory days more than a century ago?

It was no secret that Sharkey owed a lot of money to a lot of people. He had swindled thousands of people out of thousands of pounds each by using the 'fractional financing model' to build most of his apartment blocks in the city. This had made him a lot of money. But does it make sense for one individual to kill him for a few thousand quid?

'In addition to the thousands of people owed millions of pounds in all, there were some folks out there who particularly had it in for Sharkey. My sources point to three leading contenders. Firstly, Diane Ramsay. I'm told that she was Lania Sharkey's secret partner and lover? Why were they talking about a life insurance policy and a urine sample at the hospital? Which makes Lania a suspect as well. And there's Tom Wood as well, who runs Frankie's nightclub. I received some information to suggest that somebody had been blackmailing him. Could that somebody be Sharkey?'

'We need motive Sanjay. People don't just get murdered for nothing you know.'

'Here's my take Steve. Lania wants out of the relationship with Sharkey. No surprise there. She came to the UK to escape from something, fell in love with Diane. Married Sharkey for his money. And now gets to inherit that money. That's motive, no?'

'Maybe, but my IT whizz Jane Wilson told me that the Panama marriage papers were invalid and that Lania and Diane are aware of that?'

'Hence the life insurance. As for Diane, she seems to have a psychological stranglehold on Lania and will now get her into a civil partnership to get her hands on some of that dough, I guess.'

'And Tom?'

'Less certain. Sharkey knows about the illegal shenanigans at his club so he could have been blackmailing him. Somebody was blackmailing Tom, that's for sure.'

'It's a start. But it's not much to go on.'

'Finally, there's this strange business deal with Mr. Zhang, a Beijing-based investor who now owns half of Sharkey's companies, but without the liabilities. Don't know how that's possible. I got this information from the recently fired personal assistant of Andy Backland, Sharkey's lawyer. Guess she has a bit of a grudge against her former employer.'

'I'll get Jane to work more on that one, thanks. Jane Wilson. Salt of the earth. She's the best, you know. She knows the truth behind my temporary suspension. She knows that it was DCI McCartney who effed up, big time with that search warrant. The bumbling idiot.'

'Good that you've still got a reliable contact inside the force.'

'Then again,' says Steve. 'There's another possibility in all this mess. Sharkey could have just died from Covid. After all, he was suffering from a chronic asthma condition.'

Seven

Monday early afternoon, November 16, 2020, Coopers Bank, Hanover Street, central Liverpool

Lania had always known what to do if this ever happened. She hadn't wanted this, but something inside had told her that it was inevitable.

Her husband Luke Sharkey, like his business dealings, had always been a complex man. Some days she felt he loved her. More often he seemed as he'd really despised her. And now he was dead. He'd always had the upper hand. He'd always been one step ahead of the game. One step ahead of his business partners and his investors, as well. And one step ahead of her. But not now. Now it was her time. Lania time. Finally. After all that suffering.

She deserved this, she thought. She'd worked for this. She'd tried to save him from himself but failed. He thought he could outsmart all the others. But he was too stubborn. That killed him in the end. DB, she called him. DB, short for donkey brain, he was so stubborn. Then again, she could have called him FB, for foxy brain, as he was so sly and calculating. What the hell. He was dead now, and she had to act fast.

Coming out of Coopers Bank on Hanover Street she took out her phone and hand-dialled a number that she knew by heart. It wasn't Diane, her lover, she was calling. It wasn't even a national UK number. The international code was fifty-eight, for Venezuela.

PART TWO
SUMMER 1995 TO AUTUMN 2020

Eight

Summer 1995, Wan Chai, Hong Kong

Vanessa had taken up position next to the Wan Chai Police Headquarters, a solid, whitewashed building with square pillars and breezy verandas. The home of the Royal Hong Kong Police.

She spat on the coin again. She wasn't going to back down. Not now, not having gone this far. In for a Hong Kong penny, she thought, in for a Hong Kong Pound, except that it was a Hong Kong dollar coin she was spitting on. Just shows how pathetic the British are. They weren't even able to impose their sterling penny and pounds on us, after one hundred and fifty years of colonial domination and drug trafficking.

'Do that one more time young lady and I'll have both reason and full authority to arrest you and lock you up.'

The cragged, pink-faced Welsh policemen from Cardiff in his last year of service in the British colony seemed to be serious. But WTF, thought Vanessa. There's no democracy or justice here. And no respect. All that bull about being a 'protected' British territory. It's one set of rules for them in the UK and another for us here in Hong Kong. Voting? Local representation for local people? Not happening here, is it? Unlike over there in England, in Liverpool, where Vanessa had studied for her law degree, graduating last year. It's one vote for everyone over there. Bloody hypocrites.

It's going to be so much better when we move to the new system with the great People's Republic calling the shots from Beijing, she thought. So much better. Our people ruling our people. One country, two systems. And we'll meet in the middle, in harmony. Greater China will see what great people we Hong Kongers are. Unlike these British *gweilos*, our new rulers will appreciate our hard work and effort in building our wealth, instead of looking down their big noses at us. We want change. And change is on its way. Only two years now to freedom. Nineteen-ninety-seven. Bring it on!

'You are spitting on the visual representation of our monarch who, for two more years, is also your constitutional head of government.

That, young lady, is an offence in this jurisdiction and I believe that you're doing this with the deliberate intent of being arrested. And to make a stink. For what purpose I don't know. We've treated you lot very well for almost one-hundred-and-fifty years. Never had it so good. You Hong Kongers are richer than us Brits back home. Did you know that? What more do you want?'

'Sir – yes, I'm calling you sir - because I'm trying to be polite, sir. Your queen has no right to be on the coins of my country. Has she ever even visited us? Oh yeah, once in 1975 for three short days. Great. What has she ever done for us? What have the British ever done for us? Got us hooked on opium and then opened the banks to manage and pocket the profits. And here we are, one and a half centuries later, still under your rule. Just can't wait until nineteen-ninety-seven.'

'Well, good luck with that young lady. I'm not going to arrest you because I refuse to take your bait. And in a few weeks I'll be retiring and going back to my home in Wales. I don't have the time or the energy for this. Have a nice day!'

Have a nice day! I will, thought Vanessa, pondering the future. A future when these imperial Brits get their comeuppance. Enjoy your pathetic little Welsh retirement house, *gweilo*. Our time is coming, and revenge will be sweet. Sweeter than an opium flower.

Nine

Summer 1995, Liverpool Cricket Club Ground
Liverpool College vs. The Bluecoat School

This was the day. The highlight of the cricket season. The senior eleven from the non-fee-paying Bluecoat school were playing their rivals from the expensive, private, fee-paying Liverpool College. A bit like Everton Football Club, which calls itself the People's Club, against their much richer neighbours across Stanley Park, Liverpool FC, thought Sanjay Singh who was keeping wicket, with his best mate Steve Whittley leading the Bluecoat bowling attack.

For over fifty years the schools had been able to play this fixture on the impeccably manicured grass wickets of Liverpool Cricket Club, surrounded by lush trees on all sides.

'No ball', said the umpire, a teacher from Liverpool College, stationed at the bowler's end.

'No way it's no ball. My foot was in. End of. And before you ask, my previous ball was not wide. It was in line. To the right a bit, but never wide.'

'Nobody questions the umpire in cricket please. A lesson all eighteen-year-olds like you need to learn. Mr....'

'Whittley, Steve Whittley.'

'Whittley eh. Well, bowl again then Mr. Whittley and this time try to keep in line...with the rules of the game and with the wicket.'

The umpire made a sign with his hands for the scorers to adjust the scoreboard, which gave one additional run to Liverpool College for Steve's error.

Steve took the ball and shined it once again, spitting on one side and rubbing it close to his crotch area. There was a long red streak on his white cricket flannels where he'd been rubbing that ball all morning. From a distance, it looked as though he was rubbing something else *down there*. And each time he did it a group of girls whistled from the crowd, among them one of his classmates, Joanna Bradley, a cute 17-year-old he fancied but hadn't had the nerve to ask out – yet. So pretty. Many people mistook her for the English singer and musician Sade.

She was looking sexy as hell today in those tight beige jeans and the white and red shirt of her school's girls' soccer team where she played at centre back. Steve's mind drifted to a school motto: *Non solum ingenii verum etiam virtuti,* which translates as *Not only the Intellect but also the Character* and the body, he drooled, the body. What's Latin for the body? Corpus, that's it. Nice corpus.

Walking back to the pavilion end Steve turned and began his run-up, with regular steps and increasing pace until he reached the umpire and hurtled the ball down at the batsmen. Steve was a standard medium-pace bowler, but this wicket was fast. Faster than usual. And he was angry, as he often had been these past couple of years. Increasing levels of testosterone linked to a certain level of sexual frustration, maybe. He needed relief.

He was now bowling faster by the ball, which bounced early up the wicket and over the head of the batsman, taken in an impressive acrobatic jump-and-catch movement from wicketkeeper and Steve's best mate, Sanjay Singh.

'No ball,' shouted the umpire, signalling to the pavilion end where the game scorers were writing in their scorebooks and manually altering the rickety scoreboard, which had seen better days.

'You have to be kidding. Never a no ball. Aren't you supposed to be a neutral umpire, sir!'

Seeing this commotion from the other end of the wicket and having been on the butt end of Steve's teenage anger issues more than once, Sanjay ran the twenty-two yards to the other end as fast as he could and grabbed Steve by the arm, pulling him away from his nose-to-nose confrontation with the Liverpool College teacher and umpire for the day.

'It's just a game, Steve, just a game.'

'He's biased. No surprise. Stuffed up toff. That was never a no-ball.'

'And thank you Sanjay for catching the ball in an amazing jump that would have made the great Rodney Marsh happy. Otherwise, four runs for them. Calm down, mate, calm down. Almost broke my shoulder catching that ball and stopping it from going for a four. You're a great all-rounder. But that mouth, man, zip it! We're going to need you to be much calmer and more collected when we get around to batting. Steve, you're going to have to learn to control that temper of yours.'

Fortunately for all, it was the end of the over and the umpire moved back out to the right of the wicket, away from Steve, as the bowling switched ends.

A couple of overs later the players left the field for the four pm tea break. Liverpool College had finished their fifty-over limit and had set Bluecoat one-hundred-and-eighty runs to win. Steve was still arguing with the Liverpool College umpire as he arrived at the Pavilion.

On seeing Joanna, his eyes lit up and a teenage grin came out on his slightly spotty face. 'Hi there Joanna. Great of you to come. Will you be sticking around for the next innings? I'm opening the batting with Sanjay. We'll be going for broke.'

'Well,' replied Joanna, 'we might, but if you let that temper get in the way you'll be given a red card before you even get to the crease.'

'No red cards in cricket Joanna, not like in football. Not yet anyway.'

'Yeah, but that doesn't give you a *carte blanche* to swear and curse at the other school's umpire. Looked like a wide from the position Nick and us girls saw it. I thought you'd be a little more poised and calmer like your twin brother Nick. After all, you're identical. In all the time I've known Nick, I've never heard him raise his voice in anger or swear, unlike you.'

'Nick? Didn't know he was here. Yeah, well, we're different. Very different in fact. Much more than meets the eye'

'Guess so. Different vibes, I guess. Less tension. He's not like you at all. Even though you're supposed to be the same, genetically speaking that is.'

As they were speaking Nick arrived, carrying a cricket bat. 'There you go, bro. Brand new. Mum asked me to bring it down for you. Early birthday present from the folks.'

'Thanks, bro. Very timely. I'll go out there and score a ton with it. What did they give you?'

'The usual.'

'Reams of sheet music?'

'How did you guess? Yep, bro, very happy with that.'

After the tea break Sanjay and Steve went out as the opening batsmen, Steve proudly wielding his new cricket bat as if his life depended on it.

First ball. Steve to face. The Liverpool College teacher umpire was staring down as the ball was bowled. Steve lunged with his bat, but the ball bounced and swerved.

'Howzat!' cried the bowler.

Taking his time, the umpire raised his arm and stuck one finger up. That meant only one thing. Steve was out on his first ball. A golden duck.

'Lbw,' the umpire shouted. Leg-before-wicket. Steve started to walk. He had no choice. First ball. Golden duck. Humiliation. Dammit. With Joanna watching for the first time.

Sanjay watched from the other end of the wicket, cricket bat in hand. This is not going to end well, he thought to himself.

Ten

7 pm that same day, The Golden Duck, Chinese Restaurant, Chinatown, central Liverpool

As luck had it, Sanjay's prediction of mayhem, with Steve going nuts again, didn't materialise. But what did materialise was an amazing innings with Sanjay making his best-ever score of eighty-three not out. He won the match for his team with a six, lifting the ball high over the boundary with just two balls to spare in the fifty-over game.

For the first time in his life, Sanjay was the school hero. It felt good. So good. And Joanna rushed over to kiss him as he walked back to the pavilion. Not that Sanjay thought there was anything in it. He knew that Joanna fancied Steve, not him.

Steve was an impatient and irate young man, but he wasn't the jealous type. As the team captain, he'd offered to invite the whole team for a meal that evening in town using the cricket team's annual social allowance to finance the celebration. Being the hero of the day, Sanjay got to choose the restaurant from a somewhat restrictive list of low-cost eateries approved in the school budget. Steve was certain Sanjay would choose the Tandoori Chicken near his father's house in Wavertree. But to his surprise, Steve received directions for another restaurant, The Golden Duck, a Chinese restaurant in downtown Chinatown. Now that's taking the piss, thought Steve. The Golden bloody Duck.

The Golden Duck was both cheap and cheerful. Six Formica tables were tightly packed into a small area that would normally fit four. But what the heck. The prices were unbeatable, and the menu had a choice of over a hundred dishes. Five fake-looking Chinese lanterns adorned the windowsills, with three light bulbs dead. On each table were small glass bowls of soy sauce and hot red chili paste, with a spoon in each. There were chopsticks for the messy ones and forks for the lazy.

Entering the place, Steve saw Sanjay already seated at the table.

'Hi, Sanjay. Good choice of restaurant. Always loved your sense of humour. No worries, I'm not taking it personally. I was just giving you the chance to bat mate. You should be thanking me. And buying me a beer, for that matter.' As he said this, he saw Joanna already seated at another table to the side.

'Oh, hi Joanna. Didn't know you were coming. No soccer girls' night out then?'

'Your bro Nick invited me to join. Said he had something confidential to tell me.'

'Nick invited you? Strange. He's gone some other place in town. We took the same bus down from Wavertree. He asked me not to say anything to anyone, so I won't say anymore. Anyhow, you've got me instead. Same face, just a smarter brain Joanna…'

'You're kidding me, Steve? He's not coming? Then what's with this confidential stuff? He seemed to be confiding in me this afternoon. Wanting to tell me something important. Not that I was asking for it, or anything like that. What a lovely gentle and courteous man he is. I thought you were too until I saw this afternoon's performance. And I'm not talking about the golden duck Steve.'

'Let's talk about something else Joanna. How's your team doing? Who plays hooker, and can you introduce me to her…oh sorry, that's rugby. Forgot, you play soccer, don't you?'

'Steve, why so aggressive? I can't believe how can identical twins be so different? Bring back Nick, now.'

'Only kidding Joanna. I'd recommend the Peking Duck. They don't duck around with that do they?' Steve said, trying again to impress with his wit. 'And they do a great Dim Sum. It's a sort of Chinese Yorkshire Pudding.'

'It isn't, stupid. Shows how little you know about Chinese cuisine. Bet you can't even eat your food with chopsticks either.'

'Pass me your chopsticks. Watch me make a cricket wicket out of them.'

Steve unwrapped his and Joanna's chopsticks, stood three up, and put the fourth on top. in a delicate balancing act that lasted all of three seconds.

'Pretty good Steve. All I can say is that it lasted longer than your batting today.'

'And the girl's got a sense of humour too, I see.'

He then licked Joanna's chopsticks with his tongue, suggestively, before handing them back to her. The others laughed.

'You are seriously yuck, Stephen Whittley.'

Steve licked them again and let out a pathetic teenager giggle. Nobody at the table laughed again with him this time.

As they were discussing the waiter arrived at their table.

'Peking duck for me,' said Joanna.

'And I'll go for the Yorkshire Pudding,' Steve said.

'I'm sorry sir,' said the waiter, 'we don't have Yorkshire Pudding on the menu.'

'OK, then I'll take the Dim Sum, thanks.'

What a tosser, thought Joanna to herself...

Eleven

Autumn, 1995, Training Ground, Everton Football Club Academy

As Uncle Joe Sharkey and his sister Mary crossed the car park at Everton Football Club's Youth Academy, they stopped to watch the local TV channel interviewing the Academy Head, Ricky Clark, speaking to the camera.

'We monitor all the statistics around the boys' development. We look at changes in speed, strength, maturation. We constantly assess how quickly they are growing and link it to the percentage of their estimated adult height. We use scientific equations which enable us to know roughly how tall a boy will be. Everything is personalised. Although the programme is developed around each team, the elements of the programme are tailored around the individual. The wider objectives will be the same for every player: to get faster and stronger, and better tactically, technically, and psychologically. But the way they get there is different for each individual.'

Yeah sure, thought Mary Sharkey, Luke's mother. And just because my kid's got asthma, you're kicking him out. And yeah, and he's not tall enough either. But how tall were Alan Ball, Colin Harvey, and the great Howard Kendall, those Everton greats of the past? How tall is Lionel Messi? None of them taller than five foot seven inches. Luke is already five foot five and he's only thirteen years old. It's not right. It's not fair. He's managing his breathing well and yes, he has off days, but that can be dealt with.

So much for the spirit of the Holy Trinity, thought Mary, reflecting on the name Evertonian supporters had given to the great Alan Ball, Colin Harvey, and Howard Kendall.

'Oh, hi there Mary. Hello Joe', spluttered Ricky Clark, offering a handshake.

Normally Ricky was a chatty scouser, but today, sensing that the family's disappointment was verging on anger, he kept his exuberance to himself.

'All good Ricky? We've come to collect Luke.' Uncle Joe wore his neutral face, but underneath he was fuming, just like his sister Mary, who was less successful in hiding her emotions, with tears running down her face.

'No problem. I'll go fetch him.'

Ricky Clark had known Joe and Mary since Luke joined the Academy four years ago. It was Ricky who first scouted Luke on Wavertree Park when he was playing for his school under-nine team. He was an outstanding prospect, running rings around the others on the field and scoring most of his team's goals at every outing. He also starred in the Academy team regularly until last year, when his teammates started growing quicker than him and his asthma got worse.

'It's not Ricky's fault, you know Mary.'

'I know, Joe. It's just that now we're going to have to start again. Luke's not doing well at school. It's not his thing. Four nights a week down training here have left him way behind his classmates, Joe.'

'Don't worry sis. I've got contacts. Give it a couple of years and when he's fifteen I'll have a word with some of my mates in the building trade. We'll fix him up with an apprenticeship. He'll adapt. He's a good lad. Takes after his uncle, I can see that.'

'Get on with you Joe. But thanks. I appreciate it. Pub lunch this weekend?'

'That'll be great Mary. And bring Luke. I'll let him have a swig of my beer. That'll cheer him up.'

'No you won't Joe, he's only thirteen.'

Twelve

Spring, 2005, Liverpool City Council Mayor's Office

Don Ferguson, the Mayor of the City of Liverpool, loved his office. There was no better place to be, even with the horizontal rain pelting and rattling the old nineteenth-century windowpanes. With an impressive array of faux Victorian paintings adorning the walls, he wanted his office to exude power and influence to mirror his own burly frame and big, manipulative smile.

Located on the top floor of the grade one listed Cunard Building on the waterfront at the Pier Head, the Mayor's office boasted a magnificent view across the river Mersey. It formed part of the Three Graces along with the Liver Building and the Port of Liverpool Building.

Back in its heyday, the Cunard building would welcome first-class travellers on their way to New York. Cruise ships still sailed from the Pier Head, though there hadn't been any crossings to America for a few decades. It was on Ferguson's bucket list to bring this hallowed nautical tradition back to his great city before he retired. Retired. Naturally. What else? Because he would never be voted out would he, such was his command and control of his political party and most of the local councillors, who backed him, willy-nilly.

One of those councillors was in the office with him right now, Joe Sharkey, accompanied by the newly appointed City Regeneration Head, Mickey Cavandish.

'I didn't tell you about the night out with the Duke, gentlemen.' Mayor Ferguson was referring to the richest Englishman in the country, the Duke of Westminster.

'You wouldn't believe this, but we took to each other like seagulls to the river Mersey. Surprised? Yeah, I was too! Never knew that the old boy was bullied at school. And for what? Yes, his accent. He spent his early childhood in Northern Ireland and had a strong Ulster accent when he was sent to boarding school, aged seven. Who'd have known? Other kids took the piss. He gave me a rendering of what it was like. Forking 'ell, he said. And I thought my Scouse was strong.'

Grunts all around. Joe Sharkey and Mickey Cavandish knew better than to interrupt the Mayor on a roll. And they'd also mastered the art of laughing in the right places.

'Me, the terrace house fat kid from Everton and the Duke. The toff and the toffee. Like peas in a pod. And he can hold his drink too.'

'Did he confirm his plans to build Liverpool One shopping mall?' said Mickey Cavandish, wanting to impress on his first day in the regeneration job.

'Sure did. This is more than a shopping mall Mickey. It's the sign that Liverpool's back. Reformed, and not afraid to stand tall. This will be the Duke's biggest single investment. Total value of one billion pounds. Think about it. Thanks mainly to yours truly. And it will be finished just as we kick off our 2008 European Capital of Culture celebrations.

And guess what? The Duke's family name is Cavendish, same as yours Mickey, but with an 'e'. You're not a bastardised relation, are you? Haha! Mickey. All self-respecting aristocratic families have some bastards in the family, you know.'

'I'll consult my family tree Mayor, but I don't think there's any connection.'

'It's great to hear that we've got the Duke on our side,' interjected Joe Sharkey, 'but remember what you said at the last council meeting: it's all about getting money into our city and into the hands of the people in the city. Your words, and fine words too.'

'They are. And this is just the beginning. We still have a lot of eyesores in the centre, which also means lots of opportunities, gentlemen. Our Liverpool One project needs some more upmarket folk in the neighbourhood. That's why I hired you, Mickey. To find them, our investors for the future. The new Dukes. For the city, for our people.

It's all about the three Rs gentlemen, Regeneration, Renovation, and Renewal. And for you and me gentlemen, let me add a fourth: Reward. We've worked hard for this moment, and we deserve our cut. It's all above board, at least in my mind it is.

But first, we need the press on our side. There's a rookie reporter at the *Post* called Sanjay Singh. Ticks all the right boxes. Dad was the poor sod brought in to liquidate the national GiroPostalBank in the nineties.

Remember that? He's a smart kid. Studied journalism at the University of Liverpool. He's going to interview you, Mickey, first. Let's get him on our side. Keep it simple. Main messages: Liverpool development for Liverpudlians. Keeping the silver in the family chest. Charity begins at home, and all that.

These next years will be busy times for us all gentlemen. We need to be smart. Now let's get on it.'

Thirteen

Liverpool Post, May 4, 2005

Liverpool One construction begins with new City Regeneration Head Mickey Cavandish nominated

As many of our cherished red readers celebrate Liverpool FC's stunning comeback over AC Milan last week to win the European Champions League, city Mayor Don Ferguson today announced some more great news. The landmark development called Liverpool One, financed by the Grovesnor Group, kicked off today with the laying of the foundation stone by the Group's owner, the Duke of Westminster.

The Mayor said 'The name has been chosen after months of intensive marketing research to find a short and snappy brand label for what is Europe's biggest retail project.

Liverpool One is the most important development in our city centre for more than forty years. And as a born and bred Liverpudlian I am more than proud to say that it will deliver a shopping, residential, and leisure environment that few other cities can match.

Oh, and being a blue, I should also inform the city's toffees that Everton FC will be opening its second branded goods outlet in Liverpool One, named Everton Two.'

The Mayor's sense of humour was not lost on attendees at the ceremony, with half containing their laughter as the other half groaned.

Mayor Ferguson also announced the appointment of Michael Cavandish to the newly created position of City Regeneration Head. Michael 'Mickey' Cavandish's role will be to go after inward investment from all around the world to re-develop the blighted areas around Liverpool One, focusing primarily on the Ropewalks and the Baltic Triangle areas before expanding further afield.

A Liverpool native, Cavandish previously successfully managed similar regeneration schemes in Manchester and brings with him a strong network of wealthy connections in south-east-Asia and from the rapidly emerging economy of the People's Republic of China.

Sanjay Singh, staff writer.

Following the press conference, Mickey Cavandish offered to take Sanjay for a meal at the Golden Duck restaurant in Chinatown. Sanjay got into Mickey's car for the short ride, unaware of his employer's internal rules that forbid staff to accept such offers from city officials.

Entering the Golden Duck Sanjay was immediately struck by how it had changed since he was last here as a schoolkid with his best mate Steve Whittley. It was all open space now, and you could see the chef working at his wok in the kitchen. No more Formica tables. No more cheesy Chinese lanterns. No more knives and forks on the now spaced-out tables, only chopsticks.

'Now, young man, there's no question. I'll be paying this evening. No worries. Let's call this a private dinner between two friends,' Cavandish said as they sat down.

'That's very kind of you Mr. Cavandish.'

'Call me Mickey. Can I call you Sanj?'

'It's Sanjay. An old schoolmate calls me Sanj. Steve Whittley. He's been in the police for the past couple of years since graduating from university. Smart guy. Wouldn't surprise me if he becomes the Chief Superintendent one day.'

'Useful contact to have Sanj. Especially in your line of work. Ever thought of becoming the *Post's* crime reporter?'

'I'd like that Mr. Cavandish, I mean Mickey. It's certainly one of my longer-term aims. Crime and fraud are my specialist fields. At uni, along with my journalism studies, I took additional courses in criminology and criminal justice. Fascinating.'

'I bet it is. Ready to order?'

Fourteen

Summer 2005, The Pumphouse Inn, Albert Dock, Liverpool

At the tender age of twenty-four Luke Sharkey had already become a snappy, impatient young man. He hated waiting. Then again, Uncle Joe had told him that this was very important. Meet me at the Pumphouse, twelve noon sharp, he'd said on the phone, adding that millions were to be made by the two of them. Luke wasn't too sure what was meant by that, but he was certainly ready to make some millions, and more. He'd finished his apprenticeship as an electrician, with additional experience and qualifications in ventilation system installation, but was still earning a pittance in his salaried job.

Located on the Albert Dock, the red brick Pumphouse Inn could easily be mistaken for a dour Victorian church from a distance. Behind it was an old chimney that had been renovated and kept in place for old times' sake. A reminder of the docks' prestigious past. As the name suggests, the building previously housed a pump that regulated the water level of the lock gate through which the Cutty Sark and other clippers entered the docks back in the day.

Uncle Joe arrived late, as usual.

'Alright, kiddo? This time you're buying. I don't think you've offered me a pint since you had that sip of my Guinness eleven years ago. And your mother still doesn't know, by the way.'

'Yeah, very funny. OK, I'll admit, I'm careful with my money. Have to be with the chicken feed they pay me for my work. I need a change.'

'And I'm here to help you make that change, son. Remember my mate Cavvy? Mickey Cavandish. He's just been appointed the new Liverpool City Regeneration Officer. He's got ambitious plans. Look over there to the Ropewalks and the Baltic Triangle areas Luke. It's still a wasteland. No change. No development. Those old Luftwaffe pilots would still recognise it. Think about it. Beautiful homes, hotels, parks, deluxe apartments for the discerning few. Now I'm on the council housing committee I can get some sneaky peeks at what's raking and shaking, if you get my drift.'

'I don't, Uncle Joe, no.'

'Liverpool's changing kiddo. Fast. In three years this city will be the European Capital of Culture. I know, I laughed too. But it's serious. Brussels confirmed the news last week. Our mayor is smarter than you think, hiring that expensive PR outfit in the European capital. Secured more money from the European Regional Development that those central government tossers in London would never have given us. Whitehall wanted to stop him from working directly with Brussels. But he went ahead and now it's payback time. For him, for me, for you. For our city. For our people.

Look at this pub kiddo. The Pumphouse Inn. A little goldmine. With all these tourists coming here to soak up our city's glorious past. They think nothing of paying for a beer at prices no self-respecting blue would inflict on his best red-nosed mates, if he has any that is.'

'It breaks my heart to say it Joe, but Liverpool FC is still better than us. Have been since the eighties, haven't they, if we're brutally honest? *Nils Sati Nisi Optimum* – nothing but the best is good enough? About time our overpaid players started living up to that motto of ours. Wait until I become chairman of Everton FC. Sack the lot and start anew. And I'm not joking Joe.'

'I know you're not kiddo. Ambition is good, like greed kiddo. But why aren't we as good? Money, kiddo, money. They've got the dough. The mouldy old effing dough. And that's what you're going to do for me. Make a lot of new dough. And this is how you're going to do it. Let me explain my plan. It's called Project Panama.'

Fifteen

Spring, 2006

Following his uncle's advice, from late summer to the end of that year, while continuing his day job, Luke Sharkey took evening and weekend classes in real estate management and property development at Liverpool John Moores University. He needed to absorb the knowledge and learn how to navigate the many pitfalls in a cut-throat business. Construction law. Zoning regulations. Freehold acquisition. Planning submissions. Forward financing techniques. Leverage. Business modelling. Rental contracts. Nothing less than the Full Monty. From A to Z and back again.

Luke was a quick learner and began to put into practice what he'd learned. By Spring the next year Luke had already opened discussions with over fifty small, low-margin business owners in the Ropewalks area of the city, just a stone's throw from the construction site of the Duke's spanking new development, *Liverpool One*.

The Ropewalks area was still a scar on the city's changing look. Weedy wasteland turned into cheap, dilapidated parking lots. Small warehouses peddling dodgy, back-of-the-lorry mattresses and furniture. Garages offering oil filter changes and new brake pads at unbeatable prices – just don't ask where the products came from and whether they're certified. A couple of corner cafés whose most profitable customers were the rats scrummaging the food waste.

Sixty years on from the war a lot of rubble still hadn't been cleared. But Luke had no time for nostalgia. The past was dead and gone. He didn't care. Not his problem. Liverpool had been screwed by de-industrialisation. And the city had even screwed itself with the docker strikes in the seventies. Screw or be screwed, that was his motto. Everton had screwed him out of their Academy. Asthma? FFS, the great David Beckham has asthma. One day, he'd become the owner of his boyhood club. Just got to make that dough quickly. And if that means screwing others, so be it. The end will justify the means.

Change in this port city was ahoy. *Liverpool One* and the town's nomination as the European City of Culture was upping the stakes. The city had always boasted a thriving music and nightclub scene, attracting punters from all over Europe. Low-cost airlines were adding flight connections each year. Amsterdam. Barcelona. Geneva. Paris. All within an hour or so to the best nightlife in the UK. And with Liverpool FC winning the Champions League again the city had again become a magnet for foreign football fans. The money to be made today, tomorrow, and beyond was so easy to smell and taste. It just needed the right business model.

Luke's plan was so magically simple he was amazed no one had yet done it. Yet he had to get the timing right.

Sixteen

Spring, 2006, Geneva, Switzerland, President Wilson Hotel, Top-floor Executive Suite

'Uncle, why won't you tell me how much this executive suite costs per night? I can find out by other means you know.'

'Nobody will tell you, Vanessa. Special favours, you see. I don't pay the prices you'll find on the internet. Our family has been customers for many years here, my dear niece.'

'Tell me more. I've never heard the full story.'

'My elder sister, when she was still a Zhang before she married your father and took the Chan family name, became a high-net-worth client of the Perrin private bank in 1979. That was around the time the China mainland began to open to us Hong Kongers. Our family was in the right place at the right time, with the right contacts. I quickly followed her and opened my accounts here. And I've never paid anything since for my stay here. It's called Swiss hospitality, with Chinese characters.'

'So why didn't you send me to one of those Swiss hotel schools after my parents died instead of the University of Liverpool to study law? I could've learned to ski. Maybe I'd have found myself a rich Swiss husband?'

Vanessa Chan's parents had died in a helicopter crash in her home city, Hong Kong when she was a teenager. Her Mum's brother, Benny Zhang, had taken care of her and tried to keep her out of trouble. Benny had never married and always treated Vanessa as a daughter. She was blessed with an extremely high IQ, which often competed with her fiery and aggressive spirit. Uncle Benny knew that, given the right polishing, Vanessa was going to be a key element in the expansion of his business empire and family fortune, as long as she learned to control her tongue.

Zhang had built a substantial Hong Kong property portfolio, mainly in the poorer Kowloon neighbourhood in the nineteen-eighties, before the handover of the former British colony back to the People's Republic. But he'd been locked out of some of the more profitable real estate deals in the richer areas of the city by a cartel he couldn't buy his way into. Diversifying, he'd become an early investor in businesses on the mainland, as the People's Republic of China opened to Hong Kongers. Now, based mainly in Beijing, Zhang held his Communist party card up high when needed, and was determined to remain close to the right people. His businesses depended on it.

He'd given Vanessa the best school education in Hong Kong and ensured that she spoke both Mandarin and English fluently, in addition to her native Cantonese. When she accompanied him to business events, he introduced her as his daughter. She played the game well. One thing her uncle hated, was cigarette smoking, probably because he'd been a chain-smoker himself before giving up, cold turkey. She promised him she'd never smoke. She admired her uncle above anyone, always remembering her uncle's mantra that personal connections – *Guanxi* - fuel the money-go-round.

'To answer your question Vanessa, it's because you're smart. Sure, hotel school would've taught you how to lay a nice table, cook a nice meal and change the bedsheets. But not to work the law, the rules and regulations to our business advantage. This is why I got you to focus on property and commercial law in your studies in England. And I'm so proud to see that you graduated with a first-class honour's degree, as I knew you would. You don't need a rich Swiss husband. I have a much better plan for you than marriage, my dear.'

Vanessa's spent the next 30 minutes listening attentively to her uncle's plan.

He had done an intensive study of property in different markets worldwide to see where the best profits could be made. Mainland China was still top of his list, but he wanted to hedge his bets and, deep down, he didn't trust the Chinese Communist party to keep allowing capital flows out of the country. Better to go offshore in property sooner rather than later.

The United Kingdom was second on his list. Over the past twenty years residential property prices in London, the capital city, had risen by a factor of six. A house in the south-east of England purchased for fifty thousand pounds in the mid-eighties was worth three hundred thousand now. The stock market could not match that. In other regions of the country, though, the increase was much lower. Zhang was betting on those poorer regions experiencing a similar boom to the south-east in the years to come. Especially the more northern cities such as Newcastle, Manchester, Leeds, and Liverpool, with a large student and young professional populations.

What's more, around one in six Brits were now purchasing second homes which they rented out. It was called 'Buy to Let' driven by southerners taking out additional mortgages on their primary residences to finance new buys in other parts of the country.

'It's all about the capital you see,' continued Uncle Benny. 'The British invented modern-day capitalism. But then they threw away their advantages through wars, colonialization, and trying to play top-dog with France, Germany, and the USA. A very short-term strategy, if you ask me. Not surprisingly by the end of the Second World War the country was completely broke. And it still is. To invest, Brits need to borrow money. And which country is now building up the biggest cash pile in the world? You got it, us. China.

The thing is Vanessa, I have so much cash I don't know what to do with it. Keep in China? Some of it, yes, but not all. Too risky. Our stock market is too young and underdeveloped at the moment. I was tempted to invest in a start-up called Alibaba. A comrade party member asked me last year. I declined his offer. Property's my business, I told him. You'll never get better returns in your new-fangled business Jack,' I told him. Maybe I'll be proved wrong, time will tell.

Zhang went on to explain his tactics for the UK property market. The key is to find smart young property developers who know and understand the local scene and are willing to take a risk. The second determining factor is that they must be cash-poor, in need of start-up funds to acquire their first freeholds and to finance construction. That's where your Uncle Benny's venture capital fund kicks in.

We give them their first credit at conditions they'd never find elsewhere. Zero interest even, I don't care. Little by little we start to tighten our conditions, like a snake around its prey. We slowly squeeze them with a contract for this, and an agreement for that until we take full control. No hurry. *Piano, piano,* as the Italians would say. We will remain strategically patient and then pounce.'

'And how will this work in practice?' Vanessa asked

'You will see Vanessa. We wait until the right opportunities arise. All you have to do is to keep me regularly informed and I'll guide you.'

'So what do you want me to do now?'

Zhang explained that he'd created a limited company based in London. Vanessa would be named Managing Director when she arrived there next week from Geneva. The company's specialty would be real estate, though Vanessa would never have proper clients, as such. Her task would be to rummage around the north of the country for the ideal 'partners'. As a qualified UK lawyer, with a London calling card and an address in Mayfair, her credibility would be extremely solid and she'd quickly build up a network of ambitious young developers.

Zhang then walked over to the balcony overlooking the Lake of Geneva, the city's famous *jet d'eau,* and further to the snow-topped mountain, the *Mont Blanc.* As he opened the balcony windows, there was a knock on the suite door.

'Ah, that must be room service. Come and join me on the balcony, Vanessa. I've ordered some champagne to celebrate our new business venture. Dom Perignon. 1995. Excellent vintage. My guess is that by the time the twenty-twenty vintage is in the bottle our plans will be coming to fruition. Here's to the future. Here's to us, Vanessa. And here's to our loved ones, above and beyond in a higher world.'

Seventeen

Winter, 2010

Luke Sharkey had spent the last four years working from his small, one-bedroom flat in Aigburth, patiently building up his portfolio of freehold properties in the Ropewalks and Baltic Triangle area of the city centre. He now owned enough freehold space to start planning his first development.

He'd finished his real estate and property management courses with flying colours, obtaining 'top-student' recommendation from the course director. His most important *learning* was simple: *Perception is the new reality.*

Sharkey had been contacted by a certain Vanessa Chan from a big Chinese investment group in response to an advertisement he'd placed in the *Financial Times*, the UK's leading business daily. The ad was by far Sharkey's biggest marketing expense to date. The full-page piece cost him over five thousand pounds. To pay for it he'd dug deep into his savings over the past years from his overtime work in his salaried job.

Perception is the new reality.

His brazen plan could not have worked better. Vanessa Chan contacted him the day after the ad ran. And you wouldn't believe the coincidence, yes, she knew Liverpool well. She'd studied law there and loved the city. She was from Hong Kong and had explained to Sharkey that since her city territory had been gobbled up into the People's Republic, she'd realised that her place was no longer there. That she was, in fact, British to the core. She was a great admirer of the United Kingdom, she told Luke, in particular the Queen. A true royalist. The Chinese investment company she represented was owned by her uncle Benny Zhang and wanted to invest in the future of this great nation by helping to finance the re-development of those once-great northern cities like Liverpool. To Make Them Great Again, she said. What better fit?

Today was a regular grey and drizzly Liverpool Monday. It was a big day for Sharkey, his first in the small office he'd started to rent in the centre, located in the Ropewalks area. Sharkey had astutely negotiated a knock-down deal at half the standard rent, tied in for the next three years.

He'd equipped the office with all the mod cons.

Perception is the new reality.

His computer was the latest, with an expensive, high-pixel flat screen. The photocopying machine was a brand-new Xerox, top of the range. He hadn't used it yet, as each copy would cost him ten pence, because he'd taken the cheapest low-copy lease option. On the office's walls, he'd hung black and white framed pictures of the Fab Four in their younger days, the *Beatles*. All the foreigners visiting Liverpool loved the *Beatles*. You couldn't go wrong with the *Beatles*.

His office overlooked Duke Street, running from the city centre through Chinatown and up the hill towards the grim, imposing, and monumental neo-gothic Anglican Cathedral, the biggest cathedral in the United Kingdom. Sharkey knew the cathedral well. Just like Paul McCartney of the *Beatles*, Luke had auditioned for the cathedral choir but had been rejected.

Rejection. The story of his life. From the choir. From school. From Everton Academy. But no more. Today was not just the day he entered his first office. It was the day that would define his success. He was ready for it. And today he was also the first payday for his part-time lawyer, Andy Backland, who had just walked in.

'Morning Andy. How's tricks?'

'All good thanks Luke. Love the new office. No expense spared, I see.'

After a little banter about the weekend's football results – Everton had lost, again, and Liverpool had won, again – they got down to business.

'Vanessa Chan sent me an email. She wants to Skype at nine am Andy.'

'Do you know why?'

'She told me that Mr. Zhang wants to re-negotiate our agreement. Seems too good to be true. She gave me the bare bones on Friday. He's ready to triple the guarantee and add cash as long as we agree to one special clause.'

'And what's that?'

'She didn't tell me.'

'So that's why I'm here, I guess.'

'That's right. Wouldn't be paying you three hundred per hour to talk footy, Andy.'

'OK, let's see what she has to say.'

At nine on the dot, Sharkey's flashy PC lit up with Vanessa on the video call.

'Hey, Vanessa. How lovely to see you. You're looking great, as always.' Sharkey sounded as if he almost meant it.

'Thanks Luke. Good morning to you both from a sunny and glorious Mayfair. I'll email you the proposed contract right after the call, but it's simple really. Mr. Zhang is ready to extend a lot more credit and put in some additional seed funds, as he calls them. A few million in fact. How does that sound?'

'With pleasure Vanessa. But what's the catch?'

Vanessa spent some time on the finer points of the deal. As always, the devil was in the detail. She then shared the contract on the screen, asking them to focus on the two special clauses on page 10:

Special clause 1: If either of the partners dies of natural causes, proven by a registered medical doctor's certificate, then the other partner shall inherit the entirety of the deceased's UK-based businesses, without recourse to any legal claim or any other legal action.

Special clause 2: If Mr. Sharkey agrees to this contract, then two one-bedroom units in the planned Walker Square development shall be transferred to Ms. Vanessa Chan's name and duly registered in the England National Land Registry.

Short, simple, and to the point.

Mr. Zhang is over seventy years old, thought Backland, and Luke is not yet thirty. And Vanessa had told Luke that her uncle was a chain-smoker and that she'd been trying to get him to quit. It's a no-brainer.

'Many thanks, Vanessa,' said Backland. We're going to need some time to go through the contract with a fine toothcomb. Can we get back to you by Friday?'

'No problem, Mr. Backland. And your thoughts Luke?'

'Thanks again, Vanessa. I'll put myself in the hands of my trusted lawyer here. We'll get back to you tomorrow latest.'

Sharkey pressed the Stop button.

'Sweet Jesus Andy! Can this be real?'

'Give me some time to go through the full details, Luke. Sure, it sounds like a deal from heaven. Let's hope Zhang will get there first. Give me until Friday.'

'No way, Andy. That's too long. Tomorrow, end of business. We've got to get this signed before they change their mind. Does Zhang know how old I am? Maybe Vanessa thinks I'm older than I am. First time I've ever been grateful for my receding hairline and worry lines. Whatever. I'm sending her a meeting request for five pm tomorrow. Be here then. Or I'll find myself another rip-off lawyer.'

Eighteen

The next day

Backland returned to Sharkey's new office the next day.

'You see I told you so. You've got to get the washing in before it rains. That's what my old Nan taught me. You lawyers spend too much time in reflection masturbation.' Luke said.

'I'm just doing my job. You know that. You must learn to trust me, Luke.'

'Only if you remain straight with me. Make me your priority client, *il numero uno*, I will make you rich. Let me explain.'

Sharkey invited Backland to 'park his arse' on the plush couch in his office. It wasn't real leather, of course, but sure as hell looked like it. *Perception is the new reality*. He offered his lawyer a coffee. A fancy *N* capsule coffee. Sharkey didn't care for the stuff himself. He preferred the instant coffee that his Mum made. Still, he served himself a *Nespresso, what else.*

Putting his cup to one side, Sharkey recounted the story of his start-up to Backland. How he'd started with very little cash of his own. How he'd been tipped off by his Uncle Joe and Liverpool City Regeneration Head Mickey Cavandish that freeholds could be made available to him both cheap and easy, on certain conditions. How the Mayor's office had helped him purchase freeholds without going through the standard auction process. Uncle Joe had told Luke all this was 'totally above board', so no further questions were asked.

Now was the time to start building. He'd found an architect and a construction company. However, the banks would need additional funds to finance the next stages. And even with Zhang's additional guarantees and cash the banks wanted more to help finance Sharkey's ambitious plans.

'I'm ready to start building, Andy, but I need you to help me access more upfront cash.'

'Well, my friend, as luck would have it you're once again knocking on the right door. The Backland door. Ever heard of *forward financing* and the *fractional investment* business model?'

'Yeah, sure. Studied it fully. Do you think it will work for our developments,' he bluffed? *Perception is the new reality.*

'Absolutely. Think about it Luke. Over the past twenty-five years the values of UK properties have increased six to tenfold. In London even more. Interest rates have fallen from the highs of the nineties. Many owners in our country are chomping at the bit to take out second mortgages using the collateral of their first homes. It's a no-brainer.'

'Carry on Andy, I'm all ears.'

Andy went on to explain that in the Middle East and Southeast Asia, with economies booming, cash was also piling up and many investors wanted to shore up their portfolios with a UK property. The British pound was stronger than it had been in years and British law surely protected their investments better than anywhere on the planet.

'Tell me how forward financing works, Andy. Give me an example.'

'Pretty simple really. A developer – like you Luke - creates an amazingly rich and beautiful video simulation of the property in question. All bells and whistles. Sparkles and marble. Frills and all. You know what I mean. The attractiveness and appeal of the online video are key. Because most of the investors will never actually visit their apartments, let alone live in them. All they are interested in is the return on their investment which must be at least eight percent, preferably ten. This is called the 'assured return', guaranteed over three years.'

'Sounds feasible Andy. Go on.'

'You hire a company that finds investors for you. And it turns out that my brother is your man.'

Backland explained that his brother had created a firm called Expert Invest, based in London. He was a former investment banker, with previous stints in both Dubai and Hong Kong, where he'd garnered a long list of wealthy investors looking precisely for this type of investment opportunity. To date, Expert Invest had secured financing for over twenty large property developments targeted at young professionals in Luton and Manchester. Turnover had doubled each year.

'Do you think he'd be interested in working with us Andy?'

'Sure, if the commission's good. Let me explain how they do it. Expert Invest has a highly trained team of talented salespeople. Most of them are young graduates in psychology from top UK universities. The commissions they earn are big, allowing them to quickly pay off their student debts and get onto the property ladder themselves. Expert Invest pays for additional training in what they called *sales-focused neuro-linguistic programming techniques.*'

'What's that when it's at home?'

'Well, here's an example from my brother's training manual. Let me read it to you.'

Andy took out his smartphone and read from a screenshot that his brother had sent him.

'In NLP words are not just words. No. There are *power words* and *magic words* to be used to elicit certain emotions and responses. Use words like *believe, change, success,* and *happiness* to invoke positive emotions. Use words like *imagine, truth, secret,* and *expose* to trigger curiosity. *Let me tell you a secret, as not many people are aware of this* is a top phrase in NLP sales talks as it makes people feel special, different, and valued. These sales techniques work like no other, Luke. The company's turnover has been doubling each year.'

'Andy, let me tell you a secret. It all sounds like a load of BS, but I'm willing to give it a try. Arrange a meeting for tomorrow at your bro's office in London. I want to meet these sales geniuses and see how their neuro psycho linguistic babble works on this scouse git, yours truly.'

'Will do Luke. You pay me.'

'Good. Time for lunch. Who's paying?'

Nineteen

The same day, afternoon

'Thanks for lunch Andy. Always love a *Mcdonald's*. Back to work now. I need your opinion on my business plan to set up one-pound companies for each development I create. We live in a great country, Andy. Just one measly pound to create a limited company.'

'Actually, that's the minimum nominal capital. It gets more complicated...'

'Whatever you say, Andy, but it's peanuts. Small fry. I'll do that for each development. If something goes wrong, what the hell. I've only got one pound to lose. All those companies will be legally separate, and I'll move freeholds from one to another.'

'All perfectly legal Luke. Common practice in the construction industry across the UK.'

'So, if I don't feel like paying the *assured return,* my dear investors would not be able to claim anything if the company managing their investment went bust?'

'Well, kind of. If the company that legally owns the development has no funds, yes. If that company owes the investor money, for example, the *assured return,* then there's little they can do to get their money back. But don't forget Luke, you'll still have to find the lawyers that will sign off on what's called the Report on Title before you reel those investors into your enchanted web. You probably learned that in night school.'

'I did learn that Andy, I did. There won't be any problem finding lawyers to do these reports. Copy-paste, mate. Plenty of crooked law firms out there. It's more of a problem finding the straight ones.'

'I understand your frustration,' Andy said. 'The law is complicated. For example, did you know that if a law firm gives bad advice the investor can claim on the insurance company of the law firm for any incurred losses?'

'That's what I mean Andy. That's our business model.'

'Explain it again please Luke in case I've missed something.'

'It's a no-brainer. Your brother finds us investors. Each of our development companies agrees to the ten percent *assured return,* over three years. We take their money upfront to finance the construction. When they're ready, we let the apartments out and pocket the rent, which we hide offshore. We manage the properties ourselves, with no third parties. As we don't pay our investors their *assured return* they have to sue our shell companies one-by-one. But by then we'll have stripped the assets out, and they'll have gone bankrupt. The only recourse left to our dear investors is to claim back their *assured return* from their lawyers' insurance companies for negligence. Nothing wrong with that. Insurance companies are loaded.'

'It's all legal, but not exactly ethical, Luke. Sooner or later, you'll create a reputation as an unreliable and somewhat devious partner.'

'Ethics, Andy? Leave them to me. By that time, we'll have pocketed enough millions to keep our beachfront mansions in the Bahamas staffed all year round. It's a failsafe plan. Let's get more freeholds secured quickly. I'll call Uncle Joe.'

'Sounds good Luke. See you at the train station tomorrow morning for our trip to London to meet Expert Invest. Seven am. We don't want to miss this one.'

Twenty

Early the next morning

Sharkey's chauffeur picked him up early the next morning in his favourite car, an Everton blue-coloured Rolls Royce Ghost, the latest model. Sharkey, as you would expect from such a successful entrepreneur and property tycoon, owned several prestige and classic cars and employed three chauffeurs. How else do we welcome all those great players from around the world that had made Everton Football Club Premiership champions for the last two consecutive seasons? Over the past three years, Sharkey had purchased some top talent for the club including Lionel Messi from Barcelona, Cristiano Ronaldo from Manchester United, and, of course, Wayne Rooney back to his boyhood club. Next up would surely be the Champions League.

'Good morning, James. Lovely morning. Trust the wife and kids are good. Did you receive the complimentary tickets for tonight's charity ball?' Sharkey said to today's chauffeur.

'We did sir. And allow me to thank you once again for your kind generosity. As my wife tells me each day, and I could not agree more, Mr. Sharkey is truly a Liverpool legend. I am so lucky.'

'Well, you know James, I'm a born and bred scouser. This is my city. Now I've made it, I'm giving back. Not that I took anything away in the first place. No, it was all down to a solid work ethic and personal discipline and to my mother. She truly believed in me.'

Sharkey wiped a small tear from his eye as he remembered his late mother, Mary Sharkey.

'See that building over there James? That was my first major development, Walker Square. Still hosting high-net-worth students from all over the world and young professionals looking for only the best accommodation in the city centre to kick off their careers and get ahead. You see, I give people what they want. Most importantly, I've always kept a level head and remained totally honest in my dealings. Honesty pays, James. A dying virtue in this day and age if you ask me.'

'It is sir, it is.'

The Rolls hugged the river and moved through the city from south to north on the dock road and up to a gleaming, spaceship-like structure right on the side of the River Mersey at the old Bramley Dock, now better known as the Sharkey Stadium. It is the most expensive stadium ever to have been built in England, with an eighty-thousand-seat capacity. Within easy access were three massive, multistorey car parks and a fully equipped sports centre, housing an Olympic size swimming pool and an indoor, artificial turf playground adaptable for many different sports. Luke Sharkey had gifted it to the city on condition that it was named after his late mother, the Mary Sharkey Memorial Sportsplex.

James parked the Rolls next to Sharkey's exclusive executive entrance at the stadium, opened the car door, and escorted Sharkey inside.

'Have a great day boss and see you later.'

'Sharkey eyeballed the lift sensor – his private lift – and it arrived in seconds. Eye recognition, what a great invention that is. He took it to the ninth floor and strolled down to his office, with bullet-proof windows overlooking the magnificent turf that had been shipped in from the Old Lady – from Everton's old stadium at Goodison Park some years ago. Same hallowed turf, different location.

'Good morning, sir,' said Maria, Sharkey's personal assistant, a stunningly beautiful, tall, long-legged woman from Venezuela. 'This is your schedule for the day. This morning we'll be doing a photoshoot with the players in front of the Howard Kendall end, the south side of the stadium. This is for a French sport daily called *L'Equipe*. They will want you and José, the manager, in front of the players, in the middle of the pitch. Then you'll be hosting lunch with the paper's wealthy owners. Not as wealthy as you, of course. From there a short helicopter flight over to Manchester to meet with that Italian-Dutch football agent you hate. Finally, this evening James will take you to the fund-raising dinner at St. George's Hall for the new Liverpool Hospital. You'll be on the top table with Steve Whittley, the Chief Superintendent of the Merseyside Police, and his wife Joanna, Sanjay Singh, the owner of the *Liverpool Post*, and, of course, Mickey Cavandish, our newly elected City Mayor.'

'Anything special I have to do?' Luke asked

'Your speechwriter will see you later about your rags-to-riches story. Usual stuff sir. You're so good at it. And let me say again how much we are all so grateful to have you as our leader. Have a wonderful day Mr. Sharkey. A blue day.'

Suddenly, without warning, Sharkey's mobile phone vibrated and rang loudly to the tune of an old UK TV cop show called Z-Cars.

'Where the hell are you, Luke. Still asleep? Come on mate, get up. Sharp. I'm here at Liverpool Lime Street station, platform five. The train leaves in 5 minutes. Get yourself down here as quick as you can.'

Needless to say, Backland had interrupted Sharkey's beautiful recurring dream of owning Everton Football Club.

Twenty-One

The same day, London, United Kingdom

Having missed the early one, Backland and Sharkey took the later train from Liverpool to London and arrived in the offices of Expert Invest just in time for their early afternoon meeting.

The offices were located near the River Thames in a seventeenth-century mews house close to Victoria Underground station. The original inside walls had been taken away. From the inside, the offices took up the space of the whole original terrace of five connected houses. Everything was white, from the outside whitewashed façade to the tables matching the whitewashed walls of the conference rooms, to the gleaming white coffee machine to the spanking new white leather swivel chairs. There was even a white canvas painting hanging on the wall from some white string. On a closer inspection, Sharkey noticed a tiny black dot in the middle of the tableau. Abstract, he assumed. Or post-modern, or some BS like that.

'Bet that's worth a million Andy,' Luke whispered 'Wonder how it would look in our Mayor's office? Shall I make an offer?'. Whenever he strayed too far away from his hometown, Sharkey became more conscious of his strong Liverpool accent. He was a control freak by nature and was uncomfortable with people he couldn't place into his smaller, northern-England world. But he was also a quick learner and constantly told himself that those who adapt quicker are the ones who survive and thrive.

'Hi there bro. Been a while. Looking good.' Andy and his brother Graham hugged in an affectionate embrace.

'Alright there la,' Sharkey said, deliberately accentuating his Scouse accent. 'Luke. Luke Sharkey. Sharkey Group. *Luxury living for the discerning few,* that's our business.' He'd created this tagline on a post-it on the train down from Liverpool.

Andy's brother Graham Backland escorted them from the plush entrance area into a large conference room.

'To begin with today you're going to follow a sales call with our top Senior Property Consultants, Vicki Sanghera, and Oli Itoji. They will be on a live video call with Aslan Shah, a prospective investor from

Kuala Lumpur, Malaysia. He's at the hot-to-boiling stage. We've exchanged several emails with him and now it's just a small matter of having him sign.'

Vicki and Oli entered the room. Senior Property Consultants? Neither of them looked a day over twenty-five. At what age do you become a Senior these days, Sharkey thought? Both could have been front-page *Vogue* magazine models. Beautiful people. And as soon as they opened their mouths Sharkey knew that they'd both benefited from an expensive English private school education. Eton? Harrow? What other famous public schools could Luke name? Didn't matter. His kids, when he had them, would go to one. Perhaps he should get them enrolled already?

'Hello,' said Vicki, 'you must be the brother. Very pleased to meet you. And you must be our next, best, and most valued client to be, the famous Luke Sharkey. Our research and profile analysis had you on our top five list already. That is if you opt to use our services as you expand your business horizons. Honoured, Mr. Sharkey.'

She's good, thought Sharkey. Very smooth. Flattery will get you everywhere. And no, I don't mind.

Oli and Vicki then summarised how they would manage the video call.

'Aslan Shah. Malaysian. High-level exec with a leading international trading company. Finished his studies in the UK some twenty years ago at Liverpool University. Now that's a coincidence, gentlemen,' Vicki surmised, with Sharkey gawping, failing in his attempt to keep his gaze higher than it was at present.

'Suggest I take the lead Vicki,' Oli said. 'In my experience, Malaysian men prefer to deal with other men in business matters. We've been here before, and I know you understand Vicki?'

'Sure thing Oli. Doesn't matter if the cat's male or female, as long as it catches the mouse.'

'We guess that money's probably not a problem for Mr. Shah. What's more, he knows the UK well. Understands and appreciated our legal system, which will protect his investment like no other legal system in the world. Is happy with the stability of our currency, though we know better. Guess he's also aware of the stamp tax discount we offer on our Luton developments?' Oli surmised.

'Sounds good Oli,' Vicki replied. 'You focus initially on these aspects and if his wife joins him then I'll chip in with the usual stuff about creating a solid financial base for their children's schooling, the world-beating British university experience, blah, blah, blah. And at the end, you can throw in the cherry-on-the-cake stuff about Expert Invest being prepared to increase the *assured return* from eight to ten percent *only for you.*'

Sharkey and the Backland brothers watched as Oli led the call with Mr. and Mr.s Shah. It was a lesson in faked empathy and trust-building. After thirty-five minutes the client had signed the contract online, via DocuSign, with the contractual obligation to transfer thirty thousand pounds sterling as a down payment on the one hundred-thirty-thousand-pound studio apartment. Two additional payments were already scheduled within the next six months. Hell, thought Sharkey, the foundation stone for the construction was not even laid yet and the contract specifically stated that the *assured return* would only start when the first tenants are in. That could be five years away. This is unbelievable. Advance cash flow. Luke was in, but he'd let them work on him for a little longer. Never good to show too much enthusiasm too soon. He'd learned that night school.

'Impressed?' Graham Backland asked.

'Not bad,' Sharkey replied. 'I'm still not convinced that it would work up in Liverpool though. Different city, different market dynamics, different starting point.'

'If I may, sir,' interjected Vicki, 'there is no doubting that Liverpool is the next Manchester. It's a no-brainer. Southern money can only go north. And foreign money will go anywhere. We connect to anyone with surplus cash. Not just people like Mr. Shah, who, for all we know, is probably out to avoid Malaysian taxes. We also go after soon-to-be-retired British doctors and other highly paid professionals who think they can manage their pension funds better themselves. The silver dollar the Americans call it. The base is massive. Liverpool will not be a problem. I can guarantee that.'

'OK, I get it. Thanks for your time. We'll get back to you as soon as we've had our specialised financial advisors analyse the business model and the numbers,' replied Sharkey. Of course, he was not employing any other advice than his part-time lawyer Andy Backland, though *specialised financial advisors* sounded good.

Perception is the new reality.

'Fine, gentlemen. Then we'll bid you goodbye and wish you a nice trip back to Liverpool. I'm a great admirer of the city myself. I love the football team and the passion of their supporters. Magic, really magic. We'll never walk alone, will we gentlemen,' Oli said, although he'd evidently never visited Liverpool.

With Backland shooting a nasty glance in his direction, Sharkey resisted the temptation of throwing a northern expletive back to Oli's face. Good boy, Luke, thought Backland. He's learning the game and adapting. He'll survive and prosper.

In the taxi back to London Euston train station Sharkey finally let out his enthusiasm. 'We're going to be rich Andy, rich. Text your bro, mate! Not too soon of course. Wait until next week. Keep him guessing just a little longer. But don't go behind my back. I've got eyes everywhere.'

'I know you do Luke and I bet Vicki does too! Think I didn't notice your staring? Ha!'

Twenty-Two

That same evening on the train from London back to Liverpool

Sharkey was feeling good inside. He'd only purchased one-way, second-class tickets for the morning train journey down to London not knowing when the meeting would end and what return train to book.

Waiting in line for train tickets at London Euston Backland said, jokingly, that he could only talk business on the train if they were in a first-class carriage. To his great surprise, Sharkey went ahead and bought two first-class tickets for the journey. The day had been a success.

They settled down, smugly, into their plush, first-class seats and opened the cans of low-price beers that Sharkey had purchased from the discount shop near the train station.

'Let's begin with offshore, my smart-arse lawyer,' Luke said. 'What does it mean and how can it help me to become stinking rich in property development?'

'We've got a two-and-a-half-hour journey and I'm going to need most of this time to explain this to you. Relax and take another sip, it's very complex.'

'I'm all ears, my friend.'

As the train pulled out of the station, Backland started the lesson. 'I'm going to call this the *Sharkey money-go-round*. I'm sure that will appeal to your ego, Luke. Our story begins in Panama, Central America.'

'The canal.'

'Yes, that's the place. Hot. Sticky. Swampy. Ugly. The safest place on earth for offshore companies. That's where we are going to create our offshore company. Once that's done, we nominate a director, a local lawyer preferably. I know a few already. He'll be our frontman, as it's important that our names are nowhere to be seen.'

'Ours, Andy?'

'Yes, Luke, ours. You cannot do this without me and I'm taking a ten percent share.'

'We'll talk about that later. Then what?'

'We are given paper certificates called Bearer Shares. Because these have no names printed on the paper, we must keep them safe. Preferably in a bank vault. Coopers in Liverpool have a lot of experience in this. They have their vaults on Hanover Street.'

'If I understand right, if someone steals these Bearer Shares they'll own my offshore company?'

'Right. We have to take this risk as it's the only way to remain anonymous and invisible.'

'OK, I get it.'

Backland continued his explanation. 'For the sake of argument, let's call our offshore company Shark Investments.'

'Nice, I like that,' Luke replied, beaming like a little kid.

'This offshore company Shark Investments purchases a bunch of dockland freeholds from Liverpool City Council. Let's say for one million pounds. The two of us then create an onshore, bog-standard, run-of-the-mill one-pound limited company based in Liverpool. Let's call this Toffee Investments. Shark sells the freeholds to Toffee for four million pounds, deferring payment until a later date.'

'That's legal?'

'Totally. Toffee Investments then asks his mates at the City Council to free up its newly acquired freehold lots for residential development, giving them planning permission. Great for inner-city development, which is what everyone wants.'

'My Uncle Joe can help there. He's on the council housing committee.'

'Exactly. With the freehold value having gone up from one to four million in that sale, Toffee Investments uses the collateral to get a loan from Coopers Bank. We then start building. In parallel Expert Invest gets the money rolling in from those wealthy foreign investors trying to hide their money from their national tax authorities.'

'I'm not giving your brother a cut, Andy, you know that.'

'I know. Expert Invest brings in around fifty million before the building is finished on the promise of a ten percent *assured return* over three years. Still with me?'

'Sure Andy, you're preaching to the converted already.'

'Toffee now has big bucks in his coffers and persuades the bank to give him an additional loan. This time the bank is ready to go for broke, let's say one hundred million, to build a swanky top-of-the-market residential building entirely in the name of the new company that Toffee creates called Fudge Investments.'

'Prince's Place, Andy. Been thinking about that lot for a long time. Think I told you about that. Prime land, right there on the river at Prince's Dock. Uncle Joe is already on to it.'

'Right. Once the first Toffee building has been finished and the tenants are in, Toffee offers to sell the freehold back to the investors. That's a legal obligation when you sell a freehold. The beautiful thing here is that there are hundreds of individual investors, and as they don't know each other they will never be able to coordinate the purchase of the freehold to the building they own. Toffee sells it to Fudge at a much-reduced price, let's say back down to the one million Shark purchased it from the City Council in the first place.'

'Is that legal?'

'Yes, of course. Fudge and Toffee are two separate, dissociated companies. It's legal so long as Fudge can prove that Toffee sold it at market value. Fudge does this by saying that no one else has shown any interest in the freehold when he offered to sell it to investors. And here's the beautiful, magical, happy ending. We take Toffee Investments into *voluntary liquidation*. We deliberately strip Toffee of all its assets and bankrupt it.'

Luke was impressed. 'And because Toffee has no money on its books, its investors cannot claim back any of the *assured return* that Toffee had no intention of paying in the first place. Ha! Beautiful, Andy. I like it. And all above board, legally speaking.'

'Correct Luke. Toffee has now been stripped of all its income-generating assets and has no money left in the coffers. But Fudge Investments, which still belongs to me and thee, and which now fully owns Prince's Place Residence, is now worth millions. And all along Fudge Investments is constantly feeding cashback to Shark Investments in Panama. Roll up, roll up for the *Sharkey money-go-round!*'

A few minutes of stunned silence followed as they both realised that this was a business model that could make them both many millions if executed right.

As they pulled into Crewe station Luke Sharkey opened his fourth can of cheap beer.

'You know something, Andy. The train is just pulling into the great town of Crewe where some of the world's greatest luxury cars were built. Think of all those majestic Bentleys and Rolls-Royces. How appropriate, don't you think, as we finalise our plans to follow in the footsteps of some of the most successful, innovative, wealth-generating entrepreneurs in our country's history? Let's have a swig of beer to that, my sneaky, smart-arse lawyer!'

Twenty-Three

Early-December 2015, Merseyside Police Office Headquarters, Liverpool

Most of Detective Chief Inspector Dick McCartney's colleagues said he was old school. A thick-set red-head with a well-trimmed mustache in his late fifties, McCartney had learned his trade on the beat in the streets of some rough-and-tumble towns and cities across the north of England's 'rustbelt' – Burnley, Blackburn, Huddersfield, Bradford, and others. In contrast to younger high-flyers like Steve Whittley in his team, McCartney had not attended university. He'd wrestled his way up the greasy pole from the Hendon Police College to where he was now with Merseyside Police. No amount of politically correct training would change him or the way he talked and acted.

His office was located on the fourth floor of the Merseyside Police HQ, a drab, red-brick building on Canning Place near the Ropewalks neighbourhood and just down the street from the Hilton Hotel. There was nothing special about the offices apart from the sunset vistas, which could be quite spectacular across the river Mersey when the sun broke through those heavy black rain clouds that regularly characterised this wet and windy city.

Circling Steve Whittley's desk he saw the photo of him and his wife. 'Lovely photo.'

'Thank you, sir. I'd like to spend more time with her, of course, but I guess I knew what I was signing up for with the job.'

'You did son, and you'll go far. Stick with me and you'll learn. Tell you what, that wife of yours will make the other WAGs at our Christmas bash dead jealous. She looks just like that pop singer my wife likes, Sade. Do you know the one? Beautiful voice. Not to mention the rest.'

'Yes sir, thank you, sir. I'll pass it on to Joanna. She's been compared to her before. Loves compliments you know. Tells me I don't give her enough. Can you believe it? Whenever I give her flowers, she asks me what I've done wrong? We're damned if we do and damned if we don't. Isn't that right sir?'

'You're telling me mate. My wife's the same. By the way, I just wanted to inform you that the powers-that-be have asked me to follow an unconscious bias course, Steve. I said I would if I knew what the hell it meant and how it could help me in my role. You did this one didn't you, a while back. What's it all about?'

'If I may say sir, unconscious bias arises when some people hold stereotypical views of other people. Like, for example, the idea that older people like you are not as good with new technology as the younger ones. Which, of course, is not true. Look at our head of IT, Jane Wilson! Living proof of unconscious bias. She gets stick all the time, and not just from younger ones. Older folk often have other inbuilt bias issues, which I'm sure you'll learn on the course. I certainly did.'

Now in her early fifties, Jane Wilson was the HQ's information technology officer. She belonged to a select group of high potential women recruits with top-class computer science degrees, hired by the force in the nineties.

'Jane,' shouted DCI McCartney to the other side of the office, 'come over here, quickly.'

Jane, who was seated at the far end of the open-plan office, walked over, in no rush.

'Yes sir? How can I help?'

'Do you think older people are better or worse than younger people with computers?'

'Is that a loaded question sir?'

'And would I be guilty of unconscious bias if I call you a spinster?'

'Well, sir, provocation sure is an effective way of getting to the root of things, as we coppers know very well,' Jane replied, visibly annoyed. 'In my view, it's not the fact that you're older that makes you worse at IT. It's just a case of your ability to learn. Most people our age never learned IT at school. You didn't, sir, did you? But I was lucky. My Dad encouraged me to study IT from an early age. He was a copper too, in Hong Kong. That's where he met my Mum. She's a native Hong Konger and we've still got family there. Oh, and I'm not a spinster sir. I've been living together with Crys for over twenty years. She'll be coming to the ball. Steve tells me she'll give his wife Joanna a run for her money as the prettiest bird in the room, sir. Middle-aged bird, that is, sir.'

'Very happy for you and Crys. After all these years, this is the first time you've told me about your partner Crys, Jane. Good for you. Anyhow, while you're both here, can you get me up to speed on Operation Croft, thanks. In my office now, please.'

Operation Croft, Merseyside Police's investigation into building and development contracts in Liverpool, was now into its second year. The previous year the Merseyside Police had received a series of reports from four city councillors who asked to remain anonymous. The Four Musketeers, as the investigation team called them, had handed over a series of credible documents potentially implicating certain councillors on the planning committee. These elected councillors were alleged to have been *less than ethical* in their allocation and approval of freehold sales to local developers. And Luke Sharkey was one of the developers suspected of benefiting from favouritism and even of bribing certain councillors, though the police had yet to find any proof.

Detective Inspector Steve Whittley had been appointed by DCI McCartney to lead Operation Croft. He'd immediately onboarded Jane Wilson for her IT skills and historical knowledge of fraudulent practices in the Liverpool property market.

Since the arrival of Mayor Ferguson in 2010, the city had attracted hundreds of millions in foreign direct investment. Successful projects included the expansion of the city's three universities, the regeneration of derelict dock buildings, and, most of all, an increasing pool of new residential builds on city centre freeholds sold by the council. The Four Musketeers had claimed that much of the land owned by the city had been deliberately undervalued and sold by the City's Regeneration Head Mickey Cavandish under 'dubious circumstances'.

It was a mess, and with only a few short years to retirement, DCI McCartney felt it his duty to weed out the grafters and bring them to justice. If this meant rocking the boat, so be it. What did he have to lose? Once retired, he and his wife would move to their seaside cottage on the island of Anglesey in nearby north Wales. They'd even started learning Welsh to better connect with the locals.

However, very little further progress had been made in Operation Croft. Outside the group of Four Musketeers, lips were sealed. It was difficult to get reliable information about who owned what in these numerous new property developments.

A lot of the builders, including the Sharkey Group, used the 'fractional' business model whereby they hired London agencies to entice investment from home and abroad. With over twenty thousand investors and no email addresses, contacting them one by one was proving to be an arduous task. Under Jane's leadership, however, the police had infiltrated social media and had already connected with some dissatisfied investors via forums on Facebook. Most people seemed more willing to open discussions on social media than via email.

Another challenge for Operation Croft was to prove that city-owned land had been knowingly sold *under* its market value and that certain councillors and officers had benefited in cash or kind from these deals. Not easy. Without breaking the law, that is. Jane could break into almost anybody's bank account, but this would not be admissible in court, alas.

'Well, sir,' Whittley said, 'I cannot deny that it's slow going. We need whistle-blowers from the inside. Apart from the Four Musketeers, our elected officials are keeping mum.'

Steve had a hunch his boss knew more than he was letting on.

'Sir,' added Jane, 'just how far would you allow me to go?'

'You know the rules, Jane. If evidence is gathered illegally, it won't be admissible in court. So don't do it and don't tell me! If you get information from illegal activity that opens doors for you to then question suspects who then give you information themselves on questioning, or confess, then the end justifies the means. Get my drift, Jane?'

'Not really sir.'

Jane fully understood what he meant but was searching for more commitment from McCartney, who was renowned for sitting on the fence. Maybe it was what all coppers did months from retirement, Jane thought. Why take any risks now?

'You won't authorise any specific activity on my part?'

'Of course not, my dear. Think I was born yesterday? You know how it works Jane. You may want to look more closely at the activities of the Sharkey Group. Luke Sharkey's uncle is a councillor. You know that already. Our anonymous sources have also revealed that he's close to Mayor Ferguson and the City Regeneration Head, Mickey Cavandish. Now get digging!'

Twenty-Four

Mid-December 2015

Five years had now passed since Luke Sharkey and Andy Backland had visited London and hired Expert Invest to find investors. In that time over four-thousand wealthy individuals had signed up from all over the world, with a big number from Malaysia, Singapore, Hong Kong, and the Middle East. They must need to escape their tax authorities even more than I do, Sharkey thought as he poured himself a coffee that chilly winter morning.

Success had been sweet. The Sharkey Group had built a portfolio worth over one-hundred-million pounds, with more to come. Construction of Walker Square development was now finalised, with only twenty units left to sell. Tenants comprised a mix of students with wealthy parents and young professionals working in the city centre.

A control freak by nature, Sharkey kept tabs on the gossip on the different residents' and investors' Facebook pages and WhatsApp groups. He'd created a series of pseudonyms which the page Admins had accepted without question. Stupid fools! Nobody seemed to suspect anything.

Knowledge is power.

His phone rang. Picking it up he immediately recognised the voice of Graham Backland, Andy's brother and Head of Expert Invest. After so many years down south Graham has almost lost his northern twang, but it always drifted back when he was speaking to a fellow northerner. Graham had called to give Sharkey the heads-up about the imminent visit of wealthy Malaysian businessman, Paul Siew. Mr. Siew was interested in purchasing up to twenty units and would be arriving in Liverpool by train that afternoon. Would Luke be able to show him around Walker Square? Of course.

Putting down his landline phone Sharkey picked up his mobile and called a car rental company located just around the corner to reserve a top-of-the-range black Mercedes AMG for the afternoon. He then spent the rest of the morning on the internet researching Malaysia, past, present, and future, trying to find out more about Mr. Paul Siew.

After lunch, Sharkey picked Mr. Siew up outside Liverpool Lime Street train station.

'Mr. Siew, Luke Sharkey. Very pleased to meet you. Good trip?'

'Yes, thank you, Mr. Sharkey. Feeling a bit seasick after two hours in that tilting train, but all ok otherwise. Great to be back in the Pool.'

'Not your first time here then?'

'Was a student here back in the nineties. Used to work in the Golden Duck to make ends meet serving a whole bunch of drunken and rude English students at the time. Do you know that restaurant?'

'Am a regular there myself.'

'Then it'll be my pleasure to invite you to dine there later if you're available. It's moved significantly upmarket, I'm told.'

'With great pleasure.'

'And after we visit your development in Walker Square, could you please drop me off at Anfield football stadium. Home of the great Reds. I've booked a tour there. Haven't been back there since they expanded. Can't wait.'

'Liverpool supporter, eh?'

'What else?'

Sharkey was very tempted but resisted. What the hell! Selling twenty units was worth an afternoon of disloyalty to his boyhood club.

'Great team. And what a history. Am a red shite myself you know?'

'Sorry. What did you say? Red shite?'

'Yes, that's what the Evertonians call us. They're just jealous.'

'Everton? Never heard of them. Why would I have? Those losers haven't won any trophies in decades.'

'Haha, Mr. Siew. See you've got a true scouse sense of humour. Call me Luke by the way. Can I call you Paul?'

'Sure, Luke. With pleasure.'

Sharkey drove the shiny black Mercedes from the train station to Walker Square. Bloody expensive car rental for less than one mile's drive. Still, *perception is the new reality.*

'Here we are Paul. Walker Square. My first development, but certainly not my last. As you can see, we're still in the final cleaning up phase I'm afraid. I'll be adding the exclusive ground floor gyms for residents soon and I'm in discussions with several luxury brands to open retail outlets as well – *Gucci, Armani, Swarovski, Nespresso,* you know, only the best.'

Entering the first block on Walker Square, Sharkey was asked to show his credentials to a heavy-set bouncer guarding the door.

'Good security. I guess you need this, Luke?'

'Only the best security for our tenants and valued investors, Paul,' replied Sharkey.

The true motive was different. Many investors and tenants had been complaining about the poor service of the management company that Sharkey had hired to run the place. He'd taken the cheapest option, ran by a mate of his, and the service was indeed appalling. Broken laundry machines for months on end, absent concierge service, uncollected trash bins, dirty stairwells, the works.

Legally the unit owners – his investors – could change their lettings agency. That was the last thing Sharkey needed as he'd already been letting some of the apartments for cash, lying to the absent, foreign owners that their places were empty. This cash-only business was working so well for him he'd hired the heavies to stop investors getting other letting agencies to show their apartments to prospective tenants. Illegal, of course, but who cared? Most of the owners had never visited their properties and never would, just like the absent English landowners during the Irish potato famine in the nineteenth century.

'That's reassuring Luke. In today's world you can never get enough security.' Paul was duly impressed. Sharkey had got some agency staff to do a cleaning blitz just before the visit, so the place was looking much cleaner than usual. Following the tour, Mr. Siew confirmed his interest in purchasing the remaining twenty units.

Sharkey then drove the black Mercedes across the city to Anfield and dropped Mr. Siew at the stadium visit entrance. On his way back to the office he spoke on the phone with Graham Backland, who confirmed that a ten percent discount would work for a cash-only purchase of twenty units.

Over dinner that evening Sharkey mentioned to Paul Siew how he loved Malaysia, drawing on what he'd learned from Wikipedia.

'So have you been to KL Luke?' Paul asked.

'KL?'

'Kuala Lumpur.'

'Of course, of course,' Sharkey said, trying to sound worldly-wise. 'Loved it there, especially that big, tall, pointed skyscraper. The Petrol tower. Impressive. And I played at that wonderful Royal Sengalor golf course overlooking the Indian ocean. Tough round. Was pleased to play to my six handicap.' Luke was getting deeper and deeper into a quagmire of lies, and he knew it.

'Is that right Luke? I didn't know that the Royal Sengalor club had opened a second course near the ocean,' replied Mr. Siew, giving Luke the benefit of the doubt. 'The one I play at each week is located right in the middle of the city near the Petronas twin towers. I'd love to invite you next time you're over. Mind you, at six handicap you'd beat me on every hole.'

'I'd love that, thank you Paul.'

After dinner Mr. Siew duly signed the contract that Andy Backland had brought to the restaurant. Effing bril, thought Luke. Walker Square, going, going, gone.

Having dropped Mr. Siew at his hotel, Sharkey left the Mercedes at the car rental place and walked back home. Shit. Petrol Tower, he thought. Something told me that was wrong. Oh well. All's well that ends well. He signed the contract. Let's hope he means it when he says he'll pay cash. That would come in handy. I could do with some extra cash in hand to help finance a few favours with my mates on the council.

Twenty-Five

Early-January 2016, Frankie's Nightclub, Liverpool

Tom Wood had come to Liverpool from his home city, Leeds, as a student in the early nineteen nineties. Back then he'd been a minor player in the local music scene promoting local bands at pubs and small venues across the city. The Liverpool music scene had remained vibrant and innovative since the Merseybeat revolution in the nineteen fifties. Tom's music idols were the eighties' bands *Frankie Goes to Hollywood, Echo and the Bunnymen, Orchestral Manoeuvres in the Dark,* and *China Crisis.* At one point he was in contention to be the manager of *The La's,* but that hadn't worked out.

By the late noughties his impresario ambitions had faded, so he'd invested his savings in Frankie's, a city centre nightclub. He held a one-third stake along with the owner of the Golden Duck restaurant and a Dock Road car dealership proprietor. Over the past years Tom had changed the focus of the club, which now catered to *generous gentlemen with a taste for the exquisite and exotic.*

Tom knew Luke Sharkey well, Sharkey being a regular at the new Frankie's. He'd purchased four apartments in Walker Square from the Sharkey Group. Luke had personally offered him a preferential price and was paying him a higher-than-standard *assured return* each month, the payback being 'special favours', most of which were disbursed at Frankie's.

Tom lived by himself in a two-bedroom unit, with six of his male and female *students,* as he called his employees, sharing the three one-bedroom units.

'Good evening, Luke.' Tom welcomed Sharkey and sat him down at his favourite table in the corner of the lounge. The stiff, button-pinned red-leather armchairs and the low, faux mahogany tables resembled those you'd find in some of London's private gentleman clubs, which was intentional. Tom and his partners wanted to create an ambiance that recalled the exclusivity of those London clubs, without the snobbier formalities and dress codes.

'Hi there Tom, mate. Alright?'

'Yep. Got a new batch of *students* in last week. There's one I'd like you to meet, Lania. She'll be waiting your table this evening. Feel free to sit her down, as always. No time limits. All part of our *luxurious service for the discerning few*, as I'm sure you know.'

'Thanks Tom. You're the man. Always appreciated.'

Sharkey took out his iPad and began to read his email. Message from Andy Backland. Hot news that the city had granted permission for his Prince's Place development, his biggest project to date. This one would make Walker Square pale in comparison. The PP development, as he called it, would block the river views of most of the Walker Square units, but who cared.

Prince's Place was Sharkey's dream come true. It would be the first development that truly belonged to him. He'd convinced his bank manager to upfront him the funds to finance the whole two-hundred-unit development. He'd used the best location of all the freeholds he owned. Unobstructed river views. Underground parking. A ground-floor gym. He's even considered having an indoor swimming pool, but the maintenance costs were too high.

His bank had taken his other freeholds as collateral and lent him a straight fifty-million quid to build the beauty. Any cash flow issues he'd have in the meantime would be solved by simply not paying the *assured return* to the investors in his other properties, just as Andy Backland had explained to him on the train. Simple business model. All legal. All above board.

Grinning smugly as he digested the news about Prince's Place, Sharkey looked up from his table to see the most beautiful, sweet and attractive face he'd ever seen. A true stunner, in every way, from every angle. But why such sad eyes?

'Hello sir. I'm Lania. Here's your usual single malt whisky and coke on the rocks. Compliments of the management.'

'Why thank you Lania. *Qué tal mi amor*! Do I detect a Latina accent in your voice? South American?'

'Venezuelan, sir. Though I spent the last few years in Panama.'

'Know it well Lania. Fly there regularly. Why not sit down and chat for a while?'

'Not sure if I'm allowed to.'

'You are, believe me, Lania. You're new, right? Sit down, please.'

Sharkey was gawping in awe. He'd met a lot of so-called *students* at Frankie's, but none so positively spectacular as this young woman. Twenty-five years old, perhaps? Not much more, surely. But such a forlorn gaze. Almost empty. A challenge he couldn't resist.

'Panama, eh. Well, I fly out there every three months. I deliver pound sterling banknotes to deposit in an account. Hundreds of thousands sometimes. I have a lot of vending businesses in the city and get cash from my laundry machines in the apartment buildings I own as well. I change the coins for notes and off I hop. All legal, by the way. The British banks don't want banknotes anymore. They say it creates too much back-office paperwork. In Panama, though, no paperwork. No back office. And no questions asked. Don't know why I'm telling you this, do you? Must be your beautiful eyes, Lania. You should come with me on my next trip?'

'Thank you, sir, but *no gracias*. I'm leaving that place for good. I'm going to be studying nursing here in Liverpool. I just need to save ten-thousand pounds for the first year's tuition, and I'll be good.'

'Call me Luke, Lania. Luke Sharkey. I'm the Chairman and CEO of the Sharkey Group.'

'Sounds amazing. Any jobs going? I was a PA in a property company back home in Caracas before the economy crashed. Problem is, I don't have my residence papers for the UK yet. And I won't be able to stomach a dive like Frankie's much longer, that's for sure.'

'Well, Lania. Let me see what I can do. Tell me about Venezuela.'

Lania and Luke talked for a good two hours.

Keeping a beady eye on proceedings from the bar, Tom Wood witnessed first-hand Luke Sharkey's genuine interest in Lania. None of the *students* that Tom had presented previously had managed to break through the icy veneer Luke reserved for most women he met.

Could this be the start of a serious relationship, thought Tom? If so, how could he make it work in his favour? I'll keep this *student* innocent and away from the main action for the moment, Tom decided. He needed to milk this situation for what it was worth. Sharkey was an important man in this city, a property tycoon with a strong network. This could be the start of something promising.

Who cares if he never got to manage *The La's*.

Twenty-Six

July 2016

Tom Wood was right. It hadn't taken long for Sharkey to fall for Lania. Whether the feeling was mutual or not, Tom didn't care. Lania had moved into Sharkey's penthouse apartment in Walker Square. Tom surveyed Lania's movements constantly and noticed that she'd also become good friends with Diane Ramsay, a downstairs neighbour. She seemed to spend more time at Diane's place than in Sharkey's penthouse.

Diane Ramsay was a doctoral student at John Moore's University. Her thesis was about 'post-colonialism and revolution in Latin America'. For Diane, Lania provided an excellent first-hand source of information for her project.

As Tom kept watch over the two, he was seeing something deeper in their relationship. There was an attraction beyond platonic. Whatever. *Que sera, sera*, and all that. Any compromising stuff that came his way would enable him to both blackmail Lania *and* curry favours from Sharkey. Double whammy. That's how it works sometimes, and Tom was not complaining.

Today, however, Lania's focus was fully on Luke, as she accompanied him on a Liverpool sightseeing tour. Luke Sharkey was her ticket to freedom, out of Tom's *student* harem and into the wild and wonderful world of a multi-millionaire. Dinners at the city's top Michelin star restaurants, and there were many in the city. Concerts at the Liverpool Arena and the Philharmonic Hall. Hobnobbing with the rich and famous at St. George's Hall. The city's high life was hers for the making and the taking.

'You know what makes me tick, Lania?' Luke asked, as they approached the river on foot. 'See that building over there. The Albert Dock. When I was a kid, it was a desolate, abandoned place. And the streets around it were full of low life. Look at it today. Full of tourists from five continents. Renovated by the city visionaries of the eighties. Now it's time for my generation to do its bit, with me at the helm,' explained Luke, never one to underestimate his belief in his own abilities.

'I can see that, Luke. I believe you and I truly believe *in* you.'

'*Luxury living for the discerning few*, like us. I've always had faith in this city. City centre living is back. It's the future. People seek out the buzz of other people. They want to connect with the intensity of this city's vitality, which is why I'm building this city's future. In less than ten years I will have single-handedly added ten thousand high-quality, well-appointed, luxurious city centre dwellings.'

'Sounds great Luke, but sometimes your English is too complicated for me.'

'No worries. The thing is, Lania, there's no real money *in* this city. It all comes from elsewhere now. My solution is to tell a story. Spin a web. Perception, you see, is the new reality. That's what I learned at night school.'

'You're a very clever man Luke,' Lania said, with pride as she held his arm.

'Thanks, Lania, you're too kind. You know, it takes more than brains. It takes a new narrative. And the narrative I've created is that Liverpool is *back*. I'm making this once great city, great again. I'm receiving investment money from all over the world to finance my dreams. My investors are loaded. They're handing millions to me, directly, with hardly any questions asked. Bank to bank. They know they won't get any of it back until these places are rented out. They're with me because I'm promising them an *assured return* that's too good to be true.'

'Is it, Luke?'

'That's the question my investors ask every day. All *you* need to know, Lania, is that I'm a good man deep down. A very good man. I provide employment for thousands of local Liverpool workers, skilled and unskilled. I'm part of that new, ethically minded younger generation of entrepreneurs who put people first. Thanks to us, our city is now on the right track. It's a case of upwards and onwards, Lania, guided by strong, upright people like our Mayor Ferguson and our Regeneration Head. You'll get to meet them all if you stick with me. But first you must meet my Mum and my Uncle Joe.'

Twenty-Seven

July 20, 2016
Liverpool Post Exclusive Interview with Luke Sharkey,
Liverpool's top property magnate

By Sanjay Singh
Readers will be aware that our City Council has come under pressure from the UK central government, which has just published a report on the alleged dysfunction of our city, especially when it comes to regeneration projects in the city centre. In this exclusive interview Mr. Luke Sharkey, the city's leading property developer, discusses both this and other issues impacting this city.

What follows is an extract from the interview. The full transcript can be found on the Post's website.

Let me say it's great to talk to you today, Mr. Sharkey.
You're very welcome, Sanjay. Call me Luke and Come On You Blues. COYB, that's our code, and Z-cars is our tune. I know you're an Evertonian, you shouldn't hide it Sanjay.

The city has given you permission for your latest top-notch development, Prince's Place. So how do you beat that?
You know Sanjay, it's not about beating anything. The way I manage my businesses there are only winners. And the biggest winner is our great city of Liverpool.

Tell me, how come your projects always seem to get quick approval from the authorities, when other developments seem to stall? Is it more about who you know in this city?
Not at all Sanjay. It's more about *what* you know. I'm a self-made man, you know that. Everyone knows that and most people admire me for it. Planning permission? You've just got to follow the rules strictly and submit the applications right. If my competitors can't do that, well, that's their problem.

And you're on the verge of becoming Liverpool's richest man?
You know Sanjay, it's not about the money. Never has been. I'm a born and bred scouser. Grew up in a terraced house in Wavertree where my Mum still lives. I believe in the people of this city. I give them work. That's my priority. If people love me for this, so be it. Second

priority? My financial backers. The people who invest in my expertise and professionalism. From London to Beijing. They want a good return on their money, and I give them that and more. Better return than the stock market in fact, which is why they believe in me. I'm legally obliged to pay my investors their *assured return*. Good old English law, the best in the world. Don't you agree?

What do you say to those people who accuse you of benefiting from insider knowledge, especially concerning the availability of city-owned freeholds for sale? UK legislation states that local authorities can dispose of land held by them in any manner they wish so long as it's sold at the 'best rate' that can be reasonably obtained. Did you pay the 'best rate' Luke? Did you?

That's a great question Sanjay. But you're asking the wrong person. You should consult the City Council about this, not me. I'm just the developer. I know you journalists are primed to ask probing questions to keep your editors happy. People are just jealous. You know that. Success brings envy, one of the world's seven deadly sins, as my Mum always tells me. Envy breeds bitterness and bitterness leads to lies. I sleep well at night Sanjay. No worries. It's all above board. You can speak with the Mayor and the city's Regeneration Head. They have no interest in anything else but the truth, the whole truth and nothing but the truth. It's all transparent. The papers are there at the Council for anyone to consult.

The UK government commissioned a report on Liverpool City Council which paints a different picture, Luke. It states that, and I quote, 'In Regeneration, the only way to survive in the city council offices was to do what was requested without asking too many questions or applying normal professional standards.' *It also states that* 'many individuals described the style in the Regeneration department as intimidating and bullying.'

Did you ever feel intimidated by the Regeneration Head at the Council, Luke?

Mickey Cavandish! Our Regeneration Head. Ha! He couldn't intimidate a wallflower. You know Sanjay, there's a fundamental problem with those bureaucrats who came up from London to write these imbecilic reports. They don't understand our city and our unique customs and habits. What do those pen pushers know about this city? Do they care about us? My developments have provided top-class, high-quality housing for young professionals as well as for thousands of students from across the world. I'm making this once great city great again, almost single-handedly. You know that. We've used Liverpool labourers, Liverpool architects, Liverpool engineers and Liverpool surveyors to build the Liverpool of the future. And now we're being asked to kowtow to these London-based mandarins? Come on Sanjay, you know that. Enough is enough.

Thanks for speaking to our readers from the bottom of your Liverpool heart Luke. One final question. What are your ambitions in the medium-to-long term?

Philanthropy, Sanjay, and charity. Two big and very important words. Most people don't know their true meanings. But I do. Money talks, but wealth *whispers*, you see. I'm whispering now, as you can hear. You're a blue Sanjay, so you'll appreciate my generosity, as will half this city. The Old Lady at Goodison Park has served her time well, and now's the moment to change everything. I'm working on a very big project in the northern area of the docks, the part that's still horribly derelict. I can't say anymore, as I'm sure you'll understand. Just count on me to do the right thing for our great city and its great people.

Thank you very much Mr. Sharkey.

Twenty-Eight

July 2016, The Steeple Restaurant, Penny Lane, Liverpool

Steve Whittley and his brother Nick were identical twins. From that same one egg. Since their teens, though, they'd tried hard to maintain different looks and images, from their clothing to their hairstyles. Steve was somewhat staid and conservative in his tastes, something his wife Joanna was constantly trying to change. Nick, on the other hand, was more adventurous, something his partner Witold was also trying to change. You need to age with grace, as Witold repeatedly told Nick.

Both Nick and Witold were teachers at Liverpool College, the very school that Steve and Nick had despised when they were at the Bluecoat School in Wavertree. Nick was the Head of Music and Witold taught German as well as Art and Drama. He'd originally come to England from his native city Munich, in Germany, as a student. Nick and Witold had been together now for fifteen years. Witold joked that in all that time they'd still never managed to have a full evening's barbecue without it raining, or at least spitting. He was amazed at how many terms the locals had for different types of rain.

Since they were kids, Nick and Steve had had their hair cut by the same hairdresser on Penny Lane, just down the street from their old school in Wavertree. For years now they'd maintained a regular three-monthly appointment at that same barbershop to make sure that their hairstyles were as radically different as possible, both in cut and colour. As they were both prematurely grey, Steve had taken to dying his hair jet black, with a police standard short-back-and-sides, whereas Nick had let his grey hair grow and wore it longer. He also kept a week-long scraggly beard, which Steve thought was as ugly as hell, but he didn't mind as it accentuated the visual differentiation between the two of them.

For many years now their customary haircut together would be followed by lunch with their better halves in a snug little one-Michelin star restaurant at the corner of Penny Lane called The Steeple. Nick and Steve had been at school with the two brothers who managed it. The menu was restricted to just five options for starters and main course, and just three for dessert. All dishes were what they called *bistronomic* British with a focus on standard English fare with a twist. The anonymous Michelin Guide judges seemed to like it, as they'd given the place a one-star rating for the past ten years.

Witold and Joanna were already seated and in the middle of a conversation in German when Nick and Steve arrived. Joanna had started private German lessons to be able to converse with her niece. Her sister had married a German baker and the family lived in a small town called Gross Gerau near Frankfurt.

'*Geschwister* means brothers and sisters Joanna,' explained Witold. 'You see, very occasionally German words are shorter than English ones. 'OK, we do have some longer ones like *fünfhundertfünfundfünfzig*. Bet you can't say that after a couple, Joanna.'

'It means five-hundred-and-fifty-five Joanna,' Nick said as he arrived and sat down. 'That was one of his chat-up lines on our first date.' Nick then proceeded to pronounce the word in German as fast as he could, showing off to Witold.

'You know something guys,' Witold said, 'just as I'll never get the T and the H sound in English, I guess you'll never get the U sound right in German, you know, the U with those two little dots on top of it. Nick, can you please pass me zee menu, thanks *mein Liebe*.'

Everybody laughed and then moved over to their menu cards to make their choices. Joanna opted for the spinach, vegetable, and truffle risotto; Steve for the oven-baked cod pie, cheddar, and parsley mash with sautéed vegetables; Witold for the Steeple's special fish and chips, fresh peas and mayonnaise; and Nick for the pan-fried sea bass with seafood linguine.

By the time they were ready for dessert, two bottles of Cab Sauv had gone down their hatches, apart from Steve's as he was driving everyone home.

'You know Nick, it was you I fancied at school first,' Joanna blurted.

'Stop Joanna. Witold's the jealous type,' joked Nick in reply.

'Then I began to understand Nick's angle and realised I'd better move over to his bro. Same chassis, different engine, you could say. And little-by-little the ugly duckling that Steve was as a teenager slowly blossomed into the beautiful swan he is now.'

'How poetic. You're bringing tears to my eyes, Joanna,' Witold said. 'So how was that first date?'

'Believe it or not, he was the perfect gentleman. Took me to the Everton-Liverpool match, one goal apiece, followed by the Grand National at Aintree. Then dinner at the Golden Duck. What more could a woman want? He even mastered the chopsticks this time. The only problem was, he made an important mistake. He forgot to ask which football team I supported. Typical red arrogance, I suppose.'

'A red and blue match drawn in heaven. How romantic,' Witold added.

'We're still together. And so are you,' said Steve raising his glass of water. 'Here's to happiness, togetherness, and to those balls and chains. *Prost* to that. And now it's drive you tipsy lot back home.'

Twenty-Nine

Sunday morning, August 14, 2016, Liverpool City Centre

Luke was excited as he walked hand-in-hand with Lania down the street. He'd taken the early train up from London, where he'd been for his monthly dinner date with Graham Backland from Expert Invest. Graham always paid for both Luke's hotel and the evening meal, so he never missed that appointment.

He met Lania outside the main entrance to the block on Walker Square and they walked down Hanover Street to hail a taxi.

'Can't wait for you to meet my mother Mary and my Uncle Joe, Lania. Nervous?'

'A little bit, yes, to be honest Luke. You need to tell me more about them before we get there.'

As they turned the corner and walked past the Novotel a voice cried out, 'Luke. Luke Sharkey, it's me, Kevin. Kevin Day. We were best mates back in the day. Remember. We were at school together. Used to come round to your place for tea in Wavertree.'

Kevin Day and his lanky, under-fed scraggy mutt were sitting next to the entrance of a discount supermarket. Kevin was inside a wet sleeping bag and beside him were a few empty cans of cheap lager beer. His face was sheet white, with a series of open sores on both his cheeks and lips. He looked a wreck, much older than his old schoolmate Luke Sharkey, neatly dressed in his snappy, tight-fitting navy-blue suit, white shirt and thin Everton-blue tie and shiny brown brogues.

'Hello Kevin. I'm Lania. Pleased to meet you. You must tell me about Luke one day. Would love to know…'

'Get away from him Lania. He could have fleas. The dog as well. You never know. Don't touch.'

Luke pulled Lania by her arm away from Kevin, whose mutt let out a small, non-threatening wimpish squeal, surprised, perhaps, by Luke's aggressive reaction.

'Come on Luke. For old times' sake. Give us a tenner mate. How's your Mum, Mary? And your Uncle Joe? Heard that he's some big wig on the City Council. I may be a bum, but I still read the *Post* you know, yesterday's edition. Look at you. You've done well too haven't you?

Tell me, does your Sharkey Group own this spot right here which I call home Luke? If so, can you give me a rent rebate,' Kevin said, laughing at his own sense of humour.

Luke grabbed Lania's arm and pulled her away from Kevin and marched her briskly down the street, without further acknowledging his old mate.

They walked faster and faster with Kevin hobbling as quick as he could behind them, dragging his sleeping bag along the wet, dirty pavement, shouting, 'I curse you, Luke Sharkey! I curse you, Luke Sharkey. You're gonna die soon. You're gonna die soon.'

As they were getting into the taxi Kevin, who'd caught up with them now, pulled the door back open and yelled at full throttle, sending his spittle over the two of them in the back seat, 'You're cursed Luke Sharkey and you'll die soon.'

Thirty

Earlier that same morning

Unbeknownst to Sharkey, when he'd picked Lania up at the entrance to Walker Square, a hippy-like-dressed woman in her mid-thirties had been watching discreetly from her balcony.

Diane Ramsay was becoming increasingly besotted by Lania. That was not her original aim. Mixing work with pleasure was fine, but she needed to control her emotions better now, as she hatched her plot.

With Luke busy and often in London, Lania enjoyed more time with Diane, a friend who made her feel better in every way. The bond between them was getting stronger.

After an early breakfast with Diane, Lania had headed back to her shared apartment rented by Tom Wood, where she kept some personal items. It was still empty. Her flatmate Tiziana had not yet returned from her night shift at Frankie's. Maybe she'd struck a home run, as they called them when the customers invited the *students* to their home or to cheap hotels for the night. Poor girl. She needed to get out of that hell hole, quickly. Lania vowed she'd help Tiziana as soon as she had the money.

Despite Luke's difficult character, Lania was grateful to Luke because he'd protected her from Tom Wood and from the full whammy of the nightclub 'chores', as Tom called them. Beyond serving customers drinks at Frankie's and having some pathetic conversations with them, Lania was free to come and go as she pleased. Sharkey must have something on Tom. Or was Tom hoping and planning for a return favour from Sharkey?

Diane had met Tom a couple of times with Lania at Frankie's and it was a true case of hate at first sight. The feeling was mutual. If only Diane had the money to support both her and Lania. The money would come sooner or later. Sure, it would. And it would come from Sharkey directly, or indirectly, depending on which of Diane's plans ended up working the best.

She just had to play for time, keeping Sharkey interested in Lania, and keeping Lania motivated to play the role of a perfect trophy wife.

Marriage would be the best option, but failing that, a good life insurance policy in Lania's name would do the trick.

Luke Sharkey reminded Diane of her stepdad. A lying sociopath who'd married her mother and had persuaded her to change her will, leaving him everything, and convincing her Mum to take out a big life insurance policy with him as the sole beneficiary.

Her stepdad was only five years older than Diane. When her mother died, he'd immediately moved with his young girlfriend to a cute little *Villetta* nestled in the Tuscan vineyards in Italy. Diane had been completely written out of her own mother's will. Bastard. Effing bastard.

Diane was not a man-hater. Her father, twenty years older than her mother, was a kind and generous man. He was a hard-working mid-level career accountant and had seen his fair share of injustice and scams. She guessed he'd known about his mother's unfaithfulness but had turned a blind eye, especially after her elder sister had died in that terrible road accident, which had knocked the wind out of him, making him increasingly inward and withdrawn.

If you can't beat them, join them, her dad used to say. Now was the time to follow Dad's advice. To step up a gear. To get what she wanted. Diane was about to become more ruthless. Like her bastard stepdad. Like Luke Sharkey.

Thirty-One

Same day, in the taxi

'Nice friend you've got there, mate,' the taxi driver said as he steered his Hackney cab up Hanover Street.

'Don't know who the hell he is. Some street bum. Destination Wavertree mate.'

'OK. With all the roadworks it'll take around thirty minutes today, ok la.'

The driver then shut the window to the backseat and turned up his radio to listen to the football commentary. The Reds were playing an early away game at Arsenal.

Lania was upset. Tears had filled her eyes. She hated conflict and was shocked that Luke could be so cold to a childhood friend. 'The man said he knew you Luke? Who is he? Tell me. Were you friends? Do you think he put a curse on you because you refused to give him money? Ten pounds, Luke, it's not going to break the bank.'

'The thing is Lania, and this is something you've yet to learn, there are winners and losers in life. Kevin Day's a loser. Yeah, I kinda knew him. Went to the same school, yes.'

'And he went to your place to eat?'

'Occasionally. My Mum felt sorry for the kid. He came from a pretty messed-up family. His mother was a junkie and his dad a wino, just like him.'

'Then you should be helping him, Luke.'

'It's no use Lania. People like that can only help themselves. He lives on those streets and he'll die on those streets. There's no hope for him. I'd put my money on his dog outliving him.'

'You surprise me, Luke. I'm seeing a side of you I don't like.'

'It's tough out there. I create work for those who want it. Kevin Day's a bum and always will be. He doesn't want to work, and never will. On top of it all, my taxes go to pay for night shelters he could stay in if he wanted to, but he doesn't, cos they don't allow drink on the premises. You've got to get real Lania.'

'OK Luke. Let's not say any more about this. But please don't forget where I come from. I can tell you, life in Venezuela is very real. So when it comes to *getting real*, I think I know more than you. I'll have you meet my family one day. Meantime, we've got fifteen minutes left in this taxi for you to tell me more about yours.'

Sharkey used the taxi ride to give a selective summary of his life and family background, explaining firstly that his dad had died in a work accident when Luke was a baby. He was lying, of course. The truth was that he and his Mum had spent six years in and out of protected homes for battered women until Uncle Joe had persuaded the authorities to issue a restraining order on Luke's dad. He'd not seen nor heard from him since. Over thirty years now. And he had no desire to renew any contact whatsoever. His mother was happy now and had never dated any other man. Good. Getting out of the cab in front of Luke's childhood home, Lania noticed that Luke made sure the driver returned him the exact eight-three pence change from the ten-pound note for the fare, not leaving one single penny as a tip. What was that old English saying, she thought? *Count the pennies and the pounds will look after themselves.* Maybe he's keeping the coins to give to Kevin Day later? Maybe *pigs will fly*, another quaint English expression, Lania thought.

Luke's Mum's place was a tastefully renovated terraced, two-up, two-down house on a street of around thirty houses, all physically connected. Built originally to house the growing community of port docker workers in the city in the eighteen-nineties, these houses had seen both better and worse times. Many terraced rows of this kind across the city had been torn down over the past forty years. Most of Wavertree's terraces, however, had survived the cull and some of them were now privately owned and pleasantly renovated, like Mary's. Each house had enough space for the owner's car in front. As Luke's mother didn't have a car, Uncle Joe had proudly parked his Everton blue Jaguar XF in the spot.

Mary and Uncle Joe were already at the front door waiting to welcome them. They couldn't wait. Must be serious because it was the first time that their precious little Luke had ever brought a girlfriend home. Mary knew he liked women because he'd told her about some of the girls he's met at Frankie's. Uncle Joe was less naïve. Being on the City Council that managed the licenses for such premises, he was aware of the *diverse nature* of the club's business. He'd been there a couple of times himself to network with the Mayor and Mickey Cavandish, though it wasn't his cup of tea.

'Alright Luke, son,' Uncle Joe yelled as if they were half a mile away. 'So this must be Lania. Pleased to meet you, love. Or should I say *Hola, qué tal?* Hey Mary, bet you didn't know your bro spoke Italian, did you.'

'Sorry about my brother Lania,' Mary said. 'Can't say I haven't heard that one before. He's like our Dad, who loved joking all the time, all the way to his grave. You've got to look on the bright side of life, haven't you? Come on in.'

The front door led straight into a spacious living room. The old wall between what was previously the two-down had gone, creating a large interior with an open kitchen at the far end. They all walked through the kitchen and into a luminous, south-facing conservatory that Mary had recently added, with the help of some money Luke had given her.

'Looking nice in this sunroom, Mum.' As tight-fisted as he was with money, Luke would do anything for his Mum. Once he'd made it bigger than big, he'd move her out of this neighbourhood into a mansion in Woolton, a leafy, wealthy suburb of the city not too far from Wavertree. She'd told him she'd never move, but that didn't change his plans.

'I still call it a conservatory Lukey. I'd call it a sunroom if we had a bit more sun, wouldn't I? Lania, bet you have more sun where you come from don't you.'

'She's from Venezuela, Mum. It's in South America. She's a manager in the hospitality industry, aren't you Lania.'

Lania was not too sure what to say, now that Luke had started to lie, again. It was becoming a habit that she didn't appreciate at all. Or had he always been like this and she hadn't noticed?

'And the best news is that Lania has accepted my offer to marry her. Isn't that something?'

'That's wonderful news son.' Uncle Joe often called him son, or kiddo, even though he was his nephew. Luke didn't really mind.

When's the wedding and where?', asked Joe.

'We haven't got around to setting dates and finding a venue. Lania's still in surprise mode, aren't you?'

'You could say that, yes.' A knot had suddenly formed in Lania's stomach. Was this good or bad news? It was certainly what her close friend and confidante Diane wanted. She'll be pleased at least. And let's face it, he'll treat me right. Look at the way he is with his Mum. Must get closer to her.

'Lania, come upstairs with me. I want to show you something.' Mary took Lania up the steep carpeted stairs and into her bedroom.

'Now are you sure you want to marry my Lukey, Lania? If so, then I have a gift for you. If not, no worries. He'll be fine and so will I. You seem like a nice girl and he deserves that. Finally.'

'Well Mr.s Sharkey, I guess…'

'Mary, please. Call me Mary. You can even call me Mother Mary, just like the *Beatles* song. Paul McCartney was brought up not that far away from here. Our Lukey always got his haircut at that barbershop on Penny Lane. He still does, but there's not much left to cut, is there? I think he just goes there for old times' sake to catch up on the local gossip.'

Lania was at her wits' end. 'I don't know what to say Mr.s, Mary. Mother.'

'Come over here. In this drawer I keep some of my old family jewelry. Look at this beautiful diamond ring. It was my great-grandmother's wedding ring. She was born one-hundred-and-twenty years ago today, can you believe it? Her husband, my great-grandfather worked for Cunard, the cruise line. At one point he earned a pretty penny you know. He bought it for her on one of his trips to America and now I'd like you to have it. You don't have to wear it, at least not every day. When you do, you can think of what a happy couple they made. Let this be your happy ring.'

Back downstairs Uncle Joe and Luke were in deep discussion about Sharkey's Prince's Place development, his biggest and most ambitious to date.

'See, kiddo! I told you I'd make it happen. Planning permission and all that. Just ask your Uncle Joe. He's your man.'

'Thanks Joe. Appreciate it. How's Mickey C?'

'Doing a fine job. Will tell him you asked after him. Maybe we should take him up to Frankie's one day. You know what I mean. Keep him on our leash.'

'Sure. I'll organise it.'

Lania and Mary came back down, with Lania wearing the ring.

'OK girls, what have you been up to. Oh, gosh. I see. Mary. You've given her great nana's ring.'

'It's better on a girl's finger than sitting in that drawer for the burglars to take Joe,' Mary said.

'Let me see it,' said Luke, grabbing Lania's left hand. 'You never told me about this ring Mum. Is it worth a lot of money?'

'That's none of your business, Lukey. I've kept this a secret from you for a reason. And now Lania will be keeping the history of this ring secret from you until you die, isn't that right Lania?'

'It is, Mary, mother. Mr.s Sharkey. Oh, and let me just say how honoured I will be to wear this ring and to always think of you, your family, and of your late husband who died in that tragic work accident when Luke was just a baby. Must've been terrible for you all.'

Suddenly the room filled with a stunned silence.

'I'm sorry,' said Lania, realising she'd touched a bad chord, 'I didn't mean to bring this awful memory back to you all on this day of celebration.'

'No worries. It's fine,' Luke said. 'We were just a little shocked, weren't we, to be reminded of that terrible period in our lives.'

'Let's have a drink,' Uncle Joe chipped in, realising that Luke had evidently been up to his old habit of re-writing his past. 'That champagne I put in the fridge should be cool by now. Let's toast your marriage and to welcome Lania into our family.'

Thirty-Two

Same day, taxi ride home

At five pm Uncle Joe called a black cab to take the young ones back to their cosy city centre pad.

Mary had tears in her eyes as she said farewell to her son and to the lovely Lania. At last he's found the woman of his dreams. So happy for him. Aw. Bless.

Lania, who'd held it together the whole day, could not stop herself from bursting into nervous tears as the taxi headed off.

Trying to console her Luke said, 'I recognise tears of joy when I see them my lovely Lania. I've got one final surprise for you today, my love.'

'I don't know Luke. Don't you think I've had enough for one day? I'd gladly say yes to marrying you in a year or so when my immigration papers are in order. But don't you think now's a bit soon?'

'Got to get the hay into the barn before it rains. With me as your husband you'll get your papers very quickly and you'll leave the life at Frankie's behind.'

'If you say so Luke. What's this surprise?'

'We're flying to Panama tomorrow morning. Business class, what else. Direct from Manchester airport.'

'*We*, Luke?'

'Yep. Take your best clothes Miss Lania Reyes and enjoy that surname name while you have it. We're going to get married. And I'll drop off some banknotes while we're down there. And then we'll go on a cruise together around the Caribbean.'

'Don't they ask for proper papers and all that? I have my passport, but won't I need some papers from the Venezuelan embassy?'

'It's Panama, Lania. Panama. Money talks down there. Money solves all problems. On both sides of the canal. Don't worry. I've got it all worked out. When we get back we'll have a big wedding. And I'll fly all your family over from Venezuela. Once my cash flow position is a bit stronger, that is.'

'Well, ok. You sure know how to surprise me.'

What Luke didn't know was that Lania was already married. She'd been wanting to tell him, but the timing had never seemed right. And now it was too late.

Thirty-Three

Later that evening, Diane Ramsay's flat

Diane opened the door to Lania, who fell into her arms sobbing her eyes out.

'What's the matter with you, my sweet. Come on over here. Sit down. Let me take those stupid high-heeled shoes off. You need a drink.'

Lania kept trembling and sobbing for ten minutes or more. Coddled into Diane's protective arms on the long pull-out sofa bed in the lounge, she spurted out something in Spanish that Diana did not get straightaway.

'Sorry sweetie, could you say that again please.'

'*Soy....soy....soy la diabla Diane. La diabla.*'

'No you're not Lania. Sharkey's the evil one, not you. Now get this down you. It'll make you feel better.'

Lania sipped the neat brandy and gradually came to her senses.

'I'm sorry Diane, but today was hard.'

'I can see that. Just take a long, deep breath and tell me all about it.'

Lania spent the next twenty minutes explaining all that had happened that day. From Luke telling his Mum and uncle that they were getting married to the news that they were flying to Panama the next day. Of course, she didn't mention to Diane that she was already married. No need. Not relevant.

'Wow, my love. That was some day you had there. You met the Fockers and now you're getting married to Lucky Luke Lucifer Sharkey. Shit, what next?'

'I followed your advice Diane to make him want to marry me. Now it's happening, I'm scared. This is what you wanted, no?'

'Yes, it is. And it will all be alright in the end. Not too happy about your month away on that Caribbean cruise. Guess I'm just jealous. Listen here sweetie. We need to make this work in our favour. He may be marrying you, but will he do it correctly and legally? He may be faking the registry office, faking the papers, paying some money on the side. Remember, he's a lying sociopath. Did he ever tell you *why* he wanted to marry you? Apart from having a trophy wife. Has he ever told you he loves you? I don't trust him.'

'I understand Diane. What should I do?'

'Go with him. Play the good wife Lania. Tell him you love him. Most importantly, make sure you get him to take out a big life insurance policy in your favour, in your maiden name, Reyes. Yes, Reyes, not Reyes-Sharkey or Sharkey. Just do that and I'll sort out the rest.'

'OK, I'll work on it while we're on the cruise. Look, I'd better get back to his flat. Not much time left to pack my bags.'

Their goodbye was loving, tender and tearful. They were getting closer and closer. Diane just hoped that Lania would survive one month away with that creep. She promised to text every day to Lania's second mobile, the secret one they used to communicate together

Back in her lounge, with Lania back at Luke's place, Diane took out her mobile. The name and number of the journalist she was about to call were already in her phone contacts but had not yet been dialled. It was Sanjay Singh, crime reporter, *Liverpool Post*.

Diane pressed the call button. She got Sanjay's automatic reply message.

'Hi, Mr. Singh? This is Diane Ramsay. You don't know me, but I know you from your columns in the *Liverpool Post*. We need to meet. I have some very important information that will certainly interest you about Luke Sharkey. Call me back when you get this message."

Thirty-Four

August 20, 2018, Walker Square, Liverpool

For the past ten years Vanessa Chan had lived in London, following her Uncle Benny's instructions to the letter. Excepting the Sharkey Group, she'd not been able to find that rare pearl, someone who desperately needed the upfront finance to kick-start a promising property development in another deprived northern English city.

On her uncle's advice, she'd decided to move up to Liverpool. The property market there was heating up fast and Luke Sharkey was right in the thick of it. Her uncle had rigorously respected his role as the sleeping partner in the business, but now was the time to get a closer grip. He needed reliable first-hand data. The only person he trusted was Vanessa.

Normally Uncle Benny and Vanessa communicated on WeChat. Today Vanessa changed tack and decided to send him an email, as there was so much she needed to tell him and she didn't want to leave out any important details.

My dearest Uncle Benny,

I trust this finds you well.

As always, I followed your wise advice and have moved to Liverpool. I'm not using any of the apartments that came with our Sharkey deal, as I need to remain anonymous. I'm subletting an apartment in Walker Square, so there's no trace back to me, nor to my alias.

It's taken a bit of time to get used to the name Julie Ma. After a lot of practice I've perfected the name recognition techniques you taught me and I glance up instantly when someone says 'Julie'. Julie Ma. That's me now. I'm there. I'm Julie.

Liverpool remains a poor, downtrodden city. It's a real sign of China's supremacy now that Liverpool would not even make it into our People's Republic's third-level city category of cities in terms of absolute prosperity, never mind common prosperity.

Can you believe it? They haven't even electrified the train line to Preston? It's like living in a museum. In the meantime, in our country, we've built more miles of high-speed train tracks than the rest of the world put together, ha!

I took a taxi across the city the other day and saw those same old run-down houses from the Victorian age, without any heat or sound insulation. One-pound shops everywhere. Bedraggled people with depressed looks on their faces. Had they never sent their gunboats up our rivers to bomb our cities, I'd even feel sorry for these nostalgic Brits.

The Mayor said the other day on TV that Liverpool is becoming the Shanghai of the West! Ha! I'm beginning to understand why Liverpudlians are known for their sense of humour.

As you instructed, I've hired the bodyguard you recommended. She's now living with me. It's incredible how many different disguises she's got. She masters every regional English accent I know.

By the way, she's chosen the name Jenny Wang for this mission.

Yesterday Jenny discovered that Sharkey is on his honeymoon in the Caribbean with an escort girl called Lania from Frankie's club he married in Panama. We know he's hiding money there. We don't know why he's married the girl though. Trophy wife, maybe?

I'll go with Jenny to Frankie's to dig a little deeper. I've already chosen my wig and high heels for the occasion. Don't worry, I practice Judo every day with Jenny, and can still look after myself pretty well.

Jenny will also keep an eye on Mayor Ferguson, Mickey Cavandish, Joe Sharkey and Andy Backland. My hunch is that they're up to something together. We need more on this.

The Prince's Place development is coming on. All apartments are in the name of the Sharkey Group, which means we now own half. It's a smart move. He's channelling all the funds from the other developments financed by individual investors into Prince's Place. We're reliably informed that he's not too concerned about paying his investors their assured return. What do we care? The legal model we've set up protects us, that's what counts.

Regarding our specific plan for Sharkey, at present he seems in great physical shape. His asthma doesn't seem too serious. I need to know how you'd like to proceed and when. Because let's face it, my dearest Uncle, and I know you won't mind me saying this, you're still in amazing shape, but, with respect, you're no spring chicken, and time awaits no one!

With all my love, your devoted niece Vanessa.

Thirty-Five

Wednesday, August 24, 2016, International Slavery Museum, Liverpool

Diane Ramsay had asked Sanjay Singh to meet her inside the International Slavery Museum at the Royal Albert Dock. She'd told him to go to a specific room illustrating the appalling conditions on the ships carrying African slaves to the Americas from the seventeenth to the nineteenth centuries.

Diane was reading a plaque on the wall which described the conditions onboard: '*The men were packed together below deck and were secured by leg irons. Women and children were kept in separate quarters and were subject to violence and sexual abuse. About one in five captives did not survive the two-month trip and was thrown overboard. It was common to see sharks following the ships for long periods of the voyage.*'

'So why meet here Ms. Ramsay?'

Diane jumped back in fright. Engrossed in the exhibition, she had not seen Sanjay approach her from behind.

'I'm sorry. You frightened me. Hi, I'm Diane Ramsay, You're Sanjay Singh. Pleased to meet you and many thanks for coming.'

'You're welcome. How can I be of help, and why are we meeting here, of all places?'

'Why meet here, you ask? Well, isn't it obvious? Slavery exploitation and empire may have finished legally, but modern slavery, exploitation of third-world countries, capitalism and globalisation are keeping billions of people in shackles. As is sexual exploitation here in our own city.'

'Yes, I'm sorry to say it does, sadly. What can I do for you?'

'Singh? Isn't that a Sikh name? You see Sanjay, you're here because *we were there*. You're a victim too. A victim of British imperialism.'

'Sorry, I don't understand your point.'

'You came here because we British were there. We were in your country, and half of the world. Don't you see how you're all the poor victims of our imperial past? I'm ashamed of my nationality, you know.'

'Try having the Indian passport mate! Bloody pain it is for my parents every time they fly here.'

'Your parents don't have British passports? I thought all Indians in this country did?'

'No. Actually, none of my family had ever set foot in England until my Dad was headhunted from India twenty-five years ago to be the Chief Financial Officer of the GiroPostBank. He made his money and went back home for a much better life than here. Smart guy. Living like a king out there now with Mum. About time I visited them, now I think about it.'

Sanjay knew underneath what Diane was getting at. He'd visited this museum many times. Each time he did it made him think about what it's like to be a successful British journalist of Indian origin working in a city with a dark past. Sure, he was deeply ashamed of parts of his country's past. But was it his problem? Today? Now?

'You wanted to talk about Luke Sharkey, Ms. Ramsay.'

'Call me Diane, please. Yes, I do. He's just married my girlfriend, Lania, in Panama.'

'Your girlfriend?'

'And he's hiding money there in some offshore account.'

'Sounds like a matter for the police. Do you have any evidence that I can pass on to them?'

'Sanjay, why am I here with you now? I would never go to the police. I don't trust them, never have, and never will. They are simply the enforcement arm of this country's capitalist conspiracy.'

'That's original. The *enforcement arm of the capitalist conspiracy*. Will tell my old mate Detective Inspector Steve Whittley about that new tagline.'

'Look, Sanjay. I understand that you don't want to take me seriously. I'm used to it, and I don't take it personally. I also know that you're always looking out for new angles to the Luke Sharkey saga. Why is it always you writing about his business in the *Post*? Is no other journalist interested in writing about the city's biggest property magnate? You're hogging him for yourself. He fascinates you, doesn't he? Because you're clean and he's dirty? He's Mr. Hyde to your Dr. Jekyll? Am I right Sanjay? Some strange psycho-play going on here?'

'Diane, I'm just a local reporter squeezing the truth out of this complex city's political and business scene. If crime is part of that, then it's my duty to reveal it.'

'We all know that crime is integral to this city. It's in this city's DNA, Sanjay.'

'DNA? Does a city now have DNA? That's news to me.'

'Luke Sharkey is an unscrupulous, lying sociopath. He underpays and exploits his workers and doesn't respect health and safety standards on his building sites. He gives backhanders to city councillors to buy freeholds at knockdown prices. He has the local bank managers in his pocket and treats them to favours in a city centre brothel that illegally employs vulnerable foreign women without the right papers. He doesn't reimburse his investors, but I don't care about that as they're all rich gits?'

'Thanks Diane. Do you think I don't know any of that? Sorry, none of that will help me write a new story. I need real, documented proof. Call me again when you've got some. Got to run now.'

'Wait Sanjay. You need to search his place in Walker Square. I made a copy of Lania's key for Sharkey's apartment. Here it is, take it.'

'I can't do that, I'm not the police,' Sanjay replied, wondering how the hell he was going to get rid of this madwoman.

'He hides cash there,' Diane continued. 'Hundreds of thousands of pounds. Lania told me where he stashes it. It's somewhere on the roof garden. One other thing you must know: Sharkey is very weird sometimes. Lania told me that each night, he locks the door to his study and speaks to himself for around ten minutes in a low voice. She'd listened in on a couple of occasions and it was as if he was summarising his day. Praying perhaps? Or speaking to a medium?'

'Are you sure it's not you, Miss Ramsay, who's speaking to a medium? Sorry, I must run. Bye-bye.'

Sanjay didn't believe a word Diane had said. He walked quickly through the other rooms of the museum. The whole place made him feel guilty and a little uneasy. There was so much to see. So much more to learn about Britain's inglorious, shameful past. He promised himself he'd go back again, and again, and again until he had read every single plaque and watched every single video.

Thirty-Six

TWO-AND-A-HALF YEARS LATER
January 2019, Merseyside Police HQ, Canning Place, Liverpool

The cold winter wind and horizontal rain made the red-brick, square-shouldered Merseyside Police HQ on Canning Place look even more austere than usual. Plans were afoot to build a new and brighter Police HQ on Scotland Road, but most of the force weren't holding their breath.

Operation Croft had stalled. Little progress had been made over the past two and half years. Luckily, this was not the only project Steve Whittley was working on.

Most new evidence had come from email and social media communications with some of the Sharkey Group's disaffected investors, monitored closely by Jane Wilson. Some investors were based in the UK, but most were in Malaysia, Hong Kong, Singapore and the Middle East.

Today's meeting was chaired by DCI McCartney, who opened the conversation. 'Looks like our new HQ buildings will be finished before we make any significant progress on Operation Croft. I'll be retired by then no doubt. Or dead.'

'Probably dead,' replied Jane Wilson, 'sir.'

'Very quick-witted. Always on the ball I see Wilson. Carry on.'

Jane spent the next few minutes describing the various social media groups that had sprung up over the past few months. Each one seemed to be dedicated to a specific Sharkey Group development company. There were also a couple of resident groups complaining mainly about the bad service provided by Sharkey's property management agency.

From these discussions Jane had been able to connect with some of the investors and get their email addresses. A small group were very forthcoming and had given her more details including mobile numbers and home addresses, but most were wary of her communication attempts. Jane was certain that Luke Sharkey was also on these sites, using different pseudonyms.

Jane began her analysis. 'The bottom line, Gentlemen, is that the Sharkey Group owes around forty million pounds in unpaid *assured returns* to its investors. The average amount owed per investor is around ten thousand pounds. Multiply this by over four-thousand investors in Liverpool and you get to that forty million. Interestingly, the Sharkey Group took out a forty-million pound loan with Coopers Bank to finance the luxury Prince's Place development at the dock, belonging exclusively to him. Coincidence?'

Steve added that Sanjay Singh, the journalist with the *Liverpool Post*, has also amassed a ton of social media postings from residents of Sharkey's developments as well as additional investors.

'It doesn't paint a pretty picture,' Steve said. 'In a number of his buildings the heating systems and lifts break down regularly along with the washing machines in the laundry rooms. Some investors have thrown in the towel, fed up with all their dealings with Sharkey. To top it all, recently he's been buying back apartments at half the price he sold to his foreign investors. Not a bad business model eh, boss. You get others to finance the building of the apartments, deliberately run them down, let the company that owes the investors the *assured return* go bust, then use another company to purchase the properties at knock-down prices. Wish I were that smart.'

DCI McCartney was not at all impressed. 'You're *not* that smart Whittley if that's all you've got on Sharkey? I need firm evidence of fraud, collusion, or corruption? Without it we can't charge any of these fraudsters. The central government report into the inner workings of our cherished city council has not had much real impact has it! Same players, same intimidation, same corruption, but where's our evidence to put them away? It's not good enough.'

McCartney was reliably informed by his friends at the Rotary Club of the latest shenanigans at the city council. Just last week, he'd been told, the council had published a weak and ineffective report about the fractional financing model, but they conveniently washed their own hands of any malpractice. Prince's Place was now finished, with Sharkey making tidy sums in rent. And he'd already secured some additional freeholds upstream.

'We need to move up a gear.'

'Yes sir, understood,' Steve replied. 'You should also know that Mr. Singh also has a source inside Sharkey's inner circle who can lead us to the cash that he's stashing in his house. Apparently, there's over one million pounds in banknotes in his Walker Square flat, built up over the past two years since his last visit to Panama.'

DCI McCartney's eyes suddenly lit up. 'Are you one hundred percent sure about this Whittley? How reliable is Singh's source?'

'We really don't know. It's a certain Diane Ramsay. She's a good friend of Sharkey's wife, we believe. Maybe even more than a good friend. She informed Sanjay over two years ago that Sharkey was hiding cash. At the time Sanjay thought she was making this up. Thought she was a weirdo.'

'Two years, and you never told me?'

'Sorry boss.' Steve hated apologising to McCartney. 'He only told me about this in passing, last week over a pint in the pub. He said that he didn't believe the source, that she was some hippy-dressed militant who spoke to him in a very condescending and racist manner.'

McCartney was irritated. 'I thought Singh was smarter than that. Bloody idiot. Every snippet of information is worth taking seriously in this case. To think that he kept this to himself for over two years. If Diane Ramsay is right, then Sharkey could have already shipped millions more in cash over to Panama. Jane, check how many times he's flown out there these past two years. And Steve, get your men ready, we're going in.'

'Going in?' replied Steve, blankly.

'Yes Whittley. We're going to search his penthouse flat. Get the necessary backup and organise it quickly. Do it quietly but strongly. Don't break anything. I'll secure the search warrant and paperwork from the judge. She's a friend of mine, no worries. Rotary club and all that, you know how the game works.'

Thirty-Seven

March 2, 2019, 7 pm, Block A, Walker Square, Liverpool

There was only one apartment in Walker Square with a roof garden: the penthouse. And Sharkey had reserved it for himself. Who else?

DI Whittley was excited to search the property. His boss said he'd sort out the paperwork and search warrant, so no worries then.

Jane Wilson's research had shown that Sharkey had flown to Panama six times in the last two years. Wonder how much he took in cash with him on each visit?

Steve's wager with Jane was that they'd find upwards of one million in the flat, whereas Jane's bet was lower, at five-hundred-thousand pounds. The loser would take the winner out for dinner at the Steeple in Wavertree. Somehow Jane knew she'd win. Gut instinct.

The apartment was on the ninth floor of Block A, Walker Square. Whittley ordered his six-person squad to climb the inside emergency stairs in groups of two. He had a key to Sharkey's place, which Diane Ramsay had given him following their meeting. He and Jane would take the lift directly. Dressed in plain clothes, he didn't think they'd arouse any suspicions. Problem was, just as he pressed the lift button, an attractive woman of Chinese ethnicity in her thirties came into the entryway and entered the lift. She seemed dressed too expensively to be a student. She asked Whittley to press the number seven on her behalf. Steve duly obliged, repeating the number seven a couple of times. He hadn't led a house search team for a few years and felt a little conspicuous to say the least. Jane remained silent.

The woman got out on the seventh floor and wished Steve a good evening. The six officers in uniform along with Steve and Jane assembled quietly in front of Sharkey's door. Steve unlocked the door and Jane Wilson entered first in the hope that the place was empty. It was.

Following the information that Diane Ramsay had given Steve, they went straight up to the roof garden, which boasted a magnificent view of the imposing Anglican cathedral to the south-east, the Liver Building directly north, and the town of Birkenhead on the other side of the River Mersey to the north-west, where a small cruise ship was docked.

It took less than five minutes to locate the stash. Sharkey had installed a deck on the roof garden with all-weather furniture. This was Liverpool, after all. Jane Wilson found four large, fake-leather briefcases inside the all-weather trunk where the sofa and chair cushions were stored. Surprisingly, neither the trunk nor the cases had locks on them. Jane opened one of the cases and was taken aback. Difficult to give an early estimate, but there must have been at least five-thousand twenty-pound notes in it.

'Boss, over here.'

Steve ran over and opened the three other briefcases. There were similar quantities of notes in each one.

'Gotcha Sharkey. You scamming, criminal scumbag!'

As Steve continued his rant, adding even more expletives, right behind him appeared the man in person, Luke Sharkey.

Nobody had noticed his furtive arrival at the scene, too engrossed in their rummaging.

'Detective Inspector Whittley, I presume?' Luke Sharkey was in his element. Arrogance oozed from both his voice and physical demeanor. He's got a nerve. We're here searching his house and he arrives, all calm and collected, knowing full well that we've just found around five hundred thousand pounds sterling in used banknotes, thought Steve. Does he know something we don't?

'Detective Inspector Whittley, my lawyer, Andy Backland, is on his way. He's already had a discussion with your boss and has informed Mayor Ferguson. For your own sake and for your career, I would urge you and your team to immediately leave my private property. Please go quietly and put the briefcases back where you found them. Thank you.'

'Mr. Sharkey, I'm very sorry to inform you that we have a valid search warrant and that I am hereby arresting you on the charge of money laundering. You do not...'

'Don't give me all that bullshit Detective.'

'You do not have to say anything but it may harm your defence if you do not mention when questioned...'

'You have no right to do this Whittley. Your search warrant is invalid.' Sharkey said. But his nerve was beginning to crack as two officers twisted his arms and handcuffed his hands behind his back.

'You will regret this Whittley. Your career is finished. No Chief Superintendent fairytale ending for you. What will Joanna think? No head table at the Policeman's Ball for her. Let me go now and I won't press charges. If you force me into that patrol car and take me to the station, then you're finished Whittley. Believe me. I know how the law works in this city. You have no right to be here, let alone arrest me.'

'Be gone with you Sharkey. I look forward to seeing you in court. I really can't wait' Steve said, nose-to-nose with Sharkey.

'You'll wish you never did this, Whittley. You'll see.'

Sharkey's threat was in vain. Three minutes later he'd been bundled into the squad car and was on his way.

With the bounty in the bag, Steve instructed Jane to remain on the premises to inspect IT equipment in the apartment and to sequester what was necessary. Steve and the rest of his team returned to HQ.

He arrived home that night an exhausted, yet a very happy man. He proudly explained to Joanna how he'd finally laid one on that swindling crook Sharkey. How this may just be that successful arrest that would give him the promotion he'd been looking for. And how, after a quick whisky, he was ready for bed, but not for sleep!

Cuddling Joanna in his arms in bed, he went out of his way to praise DCI McCartney's leadership, a rare occurrence. Yep, he belongs to the last century. Yep, he's a male chauvinist. Yep, it's time for him to retire. But for once the old fella had had the balls to go for it and to secure the search warrant. *Who dares, wins!* And today we won. Big time. Days like this make the force such a satisfying place to work. That despicable man Sharkey fought the law, and the law won. Ha!

'Well, it's past midnight, my love. It's been a good day. A real good day. And you know what would make this good day even greater Joanna?'

'No way Steve. You've not even had a shower. It can wait until the weekend. Now go to sleep.'

Steve reluctantly, but obligingly turned over to his side of the bed. He was suddenly very tired.

Just as his eyelids were closing tightly for the night, his phone vibrated.

'DI Whittley,' said Steve, yawning.

'It's DCI McCartney, Steve. Look, I'm sorry to bother you at this hour but we've got a problem. You must come to the HQ. Straightaway. Something went badly wrong Steve. You're going to have to take one for the team. Sorry. It's going to be ugly for a while, but don't worry, I'll make it all right in the end. It'll just take some time. Trust me Steve, trust me.'

Thirty-Eight

Nine months later, January 4, 2020

Luke Sharkey's appeal against an *illegal, exploitative, and inept operation by one of the most incompetent and unprofessional police forces in the land*, as his lawyer had painted the Merseyside Police's search of Sharkey's premises, took nine months to be heard by the High Court in London. Much to everyone's surprise, the High Court had ruled in Sharkey's favour. Turned out that the request for the search warrant had not followed due process, and that the judge had never signed it. All this put the blame clearly at the door of DCI McCartney, but the police remained silent on this, closing ranks.

Fuelling the fire, Mayor Ferguson had publicly criticised the police, saying that he 'regretted Merseyside Police's arrogance towards, and intimidation of, Mr. Luke Sharkey, an upright and charitable citizen doing his best for the city.'

Merseyside Police issued a statement, which read:

Merseyside Police confirms that, following an application for Judicial Review being issued by the High Court, our independent legal advice concluded that there were technical difficulties concerning the search warrant executed at Mr. Luke Sharkey's apartment in Walker Square on March 2, 2019. The head of this operation, Detective Inspector Steve Whittley, has duly been suspended from duties pending the results of an internal investigation, which we expect to publish within the next six months.

Interviewed by Sanjay Singh in the *Post*, Luke Sharkey claimed that the publicity surrounding the search and subsequent arrest had scared off investors from around the globe and led to the collapse of two of his major city centre developments and the liquidation of the companies behind them, through no fault of his own.

Later that evening on local television, Luke Sharkey explained to viewers that 'hundreds of local workers lost their jobs because of this unwarranted arrest. Thanks to police ineptitude I will now have to temporarily suspend payments of the all-important *assured return* to my many investors and partners around the world. Add to this the reputational harm to Liverpool and you might reasonably conclude that this has not been our city's finest hour. I am now going to get back to work to bring more jobs and investment to Liverpool. I've decided not to pursue the police for any additional compensation as I believe in forgiveness. But make no mistake, I won't forget!'

Sharkey concluded his interview by saying that 'nobody has delivered more to Liverpool than me in the last seven years. Let us all learn from our lessons and move forward to make this city great again.'

Thirty-Nine

January 5, 2020, Philharmonic Dining Rooms, Hope Street, Liverpool

Steve had asked to meet Sanjay in the Philharmonic Dining Rooms opposite the Liverpool Philharmonic Hall, home of the Royal Liverpool Philharmonic, which was the UK's longest-surviving professional symphony orchestra. The pub was known as the Phil. Paul McCartney had performed there as a young musician in the sixties, and again eighteen months previously.

The Phil was certainly one of the most beautiful pubs in the city, with the decoration focused on musical themes. Two of the smaller rooms were called *Brahms* and *Liszt*. About time they added a *Beatles* room, thought Steve, propped up against the ornate bar. An online review of the pub highlighted *the high quality of the gentlemen's urinals, constructed in rose-colored marble*. On his third pint already with no food, Steve had already visited them.

Sanjay clocked into the pub just before one pm.

'Hi there, no balls. Don't shoot me. I'm only the messenger.'

'You did the right thing mate. I did too. It was that gaffing idiot McCartney who effed up. He didn't even properly secure the search warrant from his Rotary friend the judge. And the force remains silent. We close ranks. Who's the fall guy, though? Yours effing truly. Yet in all this mess McCartney's still telling me not to worry, that I'll be re-instated. Should I trust him Sanj?'

'I dunno mate. Seems like the Mayor and that slimy toad Cavandish are protecting Sharkey and Backland come rain, come shine. They must be receiving backhanders. We just need proof.'

'What should I do now Sanjay? How long will all this take?'

'First things first Steve. Promise me this: Go slow on the booze! We'll have a good bender this afternoon. Joanna will understand. But that's it. No more after that. It'll only make things worse. Me and you need to start working in secret on this case. Would be great if you could persuade an insider at HQ to help as well. Jane Wilson, maybe? I'll text you a meeting time for a serious head-to-head soon when I've gathered more evidence. Meantime, another pint, pal?'

Forty

End-January 2020

When they got married Steve and Joanna Whittley had purchased a large, four-floor, hundred-year-old run-down house for peanuts in the Wavertree neighbourhood where Steve had grown up. They'd got a great deal. Nearby was an aquatic centre with two swimming pools, an athletics track and a tennis centre. Adjacent was a big public park with football and rugby posts and large green spaces for locals to have their dogs sniff and chase each other's bums. Everton legend Wayne Rooney had played Sunday football in that same park when he was a kid. Wavertree's crime rate was higher than many other of the surrounding suburbs. But this hadn't deterred Steve and Joanna.

When they'd moved in, they'd planned for a family of at least three, maybe four children. It wasn't to be. Despite everything, they'd now accepted their lot and decided they were now too old to adopt. With the house too big for the two of them, Steve and Joanna had agreed to transform it into two apartments, with the aim of renting one out for short stays.

Steve was good at many things, but handiwork was not one of them. Fortunately, his wife was much better skilled at this and had been leading the renovation work for the past eighteen months. Steve's suspension from the force had put a real damper on progress. He was at home, almost all the time. Joanna had been ruminating on a plan to get him out of the house and was now ready to propose it, tactfully.

'Steve, while I appreciate your help around the house, I think your numerous talents are better used elsewhere,' she said, over morning coffee. 'You've always loved taking our friends from other parts of the country around the city, showing them the sights. Why not become a tourist guide for a while? You're on full pay, at least until the end of the inquiry. What would you have to lose? No-one knows this city better than you Steve.'

'Me? Tourist guide Joanna? My name's been soiled in the press, my sweet. Who'd want to hire *me*, the fall guy, as a guide?'

'Steve, I know that your case is important, but the news hasn't gone any further than the *Liverpool Post*. I somehow doubt that visitors from

Norway, France, Germany, or wherever would have heard anything about you. Jurgen Klopp, Frank Lampard and John Lennon maybe, but not Steve Whittley, honest copper.'

'Yeah, I suppose you're right. Gotta say I've always enjoyed showing our great city off to friends. There's so much to see. And there's one statistic I always tell them, and that's the win rate of Liverpool against Everton over the last hundred-and-thirty years my dearest Toffee wife.'

'Not taking the bait Steve. So that's a yes then? I can book you down on the City's list of tourist guides? What's your hourly rate?'

'*Hourly* rate my sweet? Now that's optimistic. Better that I charge per fifteen minutes of strenuous effort, ha!'

'Don't exaggerate Steve! Really, how much would you charge per hour as the city's top tourist guide?'

'I'm not allowed to earn any other income while I'm suspended on full pay Joanna. Of course, they cannot stop me from asking my customers to give some coins to a charity, would they? That would look good on me, wouldn't it?'

'Which deserving charity would you consider Steve?'

'How about Everton Football Club?'

'You're so funny.'

'OK, being serious now. I'd go for Shelter. Those guys that help the homeless and people who are being abused by exploitative landlords, like City Hygge. Hell, we've got our fair share of sad cases sleeping rough in our city. Terrible. Always breaks my heart doing the city centre rounds and seeing them there in those shopfronts. There's one lad down there, Kevin Day. Probably in his late thirties, but looks sixty, poor fella. Nice man, but he's totally lost it. Has a chat with me every time he sees me. And you know what, the last time we met he was ranting on about Luke Sharkey, of all people. Says that he's always in Coopers Bank on Hanover Street. Then he told me the weirdest thing.'

'What was that, Steve?'

'That he'd put a curse on Luke Sharkey because he insulted him and his dog. He said that Sharkey would be dead within the year.'

'Weirdos everywhere Steve.'

'What he said hit me in the gut, deep down. That same gut that tells me Luke Sharkey is the most corrupt, lying, sociopathic creep I've ever met,' Steve said, getting redder in the face as he spoke.

'Let him go, Steve. You've got to let Sharkey go. Get him out of your mind. He's toxic. Poisonous. Look, I'm going to register you on that list of tourist guides and by the end of next week you'll be down at the Albert Dock starting your new temporary job. And to look good, you'd better get your hair cut. It's been a while since we caught up with Nick and Witold?'

'Yes, my love. Whatever you say, my love. Happy wife, happy life, my love.'

Forty-One

Early-March 2020, Liverpool City Centre

Steve had taken to his work as a tourist guide like a seagull to the local fish and chip shop.

That Wednesday morning Steve was with a tourist group, his tenth in so many days. They'd reached the Cavern Club on Mathew Street. Today's tour was focused on the musical history of Liverpool. Steve had quickly created a successful niche for his personalised tours. There was the Liverpool Music Tour, the Liverpool Football Tour, the Liverpool Maritime Tour, the Liverpool Wartime Tour, the Liverpool Shame Tour, and more. His wife Joanna sensed he'd never been happier in his whole life. He was drinking much less, never woke up at night, and had lost some weight. Maybe he should leave the force and focus on this line of work. Less chance of being stabbed or spat at on duty, that's for sure.

'Thank you everyone for giving generously to Shelter, a fabulous organisation trying to get those poor folk you saw sleeping rough into secure housing and new lives. *All they need is love.* Have a great day folks and come back soon!'

It was late morning and Steve had fixed a lunchtime meeting with Sanjay Singh at the offices of the *Liverpool Post* in the city centre. It was a short walk from the Cavern Club.

Sanjay was waiting for Steve at the reception. He'd booked a conference room with a screen and projector and had brought his computer with him.

'Got a lot to show the fall guy today. It should pick you up a bit as well,' Sanjay said, kicking off the meeting.

'Thanks, Sanj, but I don't need picking up anymore. Found my niche in life. Happy man I am. I'm even tempted to leave the force for good. So, what have you got?'

'Don't expect too much Steve. I've been in contact with a lot of Sharkey's investors. Remember, the ones that financed his first buildings and got their fingers burned. Turns out there's a mass of pending lawsuits out there against our man.'

'Give me the latest state of play Sanj.'

'Firstly, put yourself in the shoes of Amir Khan, an investor from Malaysia. This is what he wrote in his email. Here's the text on the screen.

Dear Mr. Singh,

Firstly, I am very relieved that someone is at last taking me seriously. Thank you! I wrote to the Liverpool Post because neither City Hygge nor the Sharkey Group replied to my numerous emails and calls.

'City Hygge?'

'Sorry Steve thought you knew. Sharkey sacked his other property management firms, Urban Snuggle and Urban Revolution, and set up his wholly-owned outfit called City Hygge. He told me that he likes the Nordic connotation. On its website City Hygge promises tenants a *mood of coziness and comfortable conviviality with feelings of wellness and contentment.* No kidding!

'Let's continue with Mr. Khan's email, up on the screen.'

I am owed over ten thousand British pounds in so-called assured return by this Sharkey crook. That might not sound like a lot of money to you, but I cashed in thirty percent of my pension funds to buy this property. Sharkey promised me a ten percent return. But I haven't received a penny from him. What a joke! My place in Walker Square has now been empty for over a year. City Hygge say they cannot find a renter. That's a joke as well. I've learned that the property nearby, Prince's Place, which is fully owned by Sharkey and is also managed by City Hygge is full. Why?

'You see Steve, Sharkey has not been paying his investors their assured return and is directing all rental inquiries to Prince's Place, which is also managed by City Hygge.'

'Illegal?'

'Yes, and no. For each development he has a different company. Walker Square Developments should be paying Mr. Khan, and hundreds more investors, the *assured return.* If WSD does not pay, then the investors must take legal action against it to recuperate their money. And if that company goes bust, then any contracts it has with investors will not be respected. Sharkey has a completely different limited company for Prince's Place. Smart guy. He plays the system close to the wire whilst remaining within the law.'

'He takes from his left, deliberately bankrupted pocket, and puts it into his right, full pocket. I'm a copper Sanj. I respect the law. It's my job to defend it. But what this con does is just plain wrong, legal or illegal.'

'Let's finish with Mr. Khan, Steve.'

I also have strong suspicions that they've been renting my place out without my knowledge to tenants waiting for apartments to be finished in Prince's Place. This is illegal, but I can't report him as my evidence is only hearsay. I've been in contact with other investors from my country and they all tell me the same story. I have done some research. The Sharkey Group has over four thousand investors in its developments. If each one of them is owed ten-thousand pounds sterling, like me, that makes forty million pounds. Can you believe that? And how is your wonderful English Law protecting us foreign investors? I'd like to know. Because we here in Malaysia now have capital and why are we investing in your country? Because we trust your old and respected English Law to protect our investments. But this is not happening. Sharkey has no respect for us Johnny Foreigners. It's a disgrace to the reputation of your country.'

'He's not wrong there Sanj.'

'Let me now show you this chart from a private Facebook page created by Walker Square investors. Mr. Khan is also on this feed, but I've replaced the names with numbers, for confidentiality.'

Investor 1

Just heard that Luke Sharkey made a clear five-million profit on a property the City Council sold him four years ago. It's true. I'll send you the link.

Investor 2

How can that happen? The crook still owes us so much money for Walker Square. I don't believe any of his promises anymore that he's going to pay us back. What can we do to get him behind bars?

Investor 1

He made the profit on what's called the 'Planning Gain'. He purchased the lot for peanuts from the City Council. That same City Council then gives planning permission and the value quadruples.

Investor 2

Doesn't that look suspicious to everyone?

Investor 3

IMO it's more than suspicious. It's downright criminal. Bet there's some high-level councillor pulling strings for Sharkey and getting paid backhanders. In my country this is how it works, that's for sure. Never thought this would happen in

England. Always felt sure that the law would protect my English investments. I was wrong.

Steve was beginning to feel sorry for the investors, They'd been scammed by both Expert Invest and the Sharkey Group. Many of them invested big percentages of their pension funds in England because they trusted English law. The Sharkey Group was flouting contractual law by not paying them their *assured return*.

'These people feel betrayed by our country's legal system. It's our job to restore confidence and prove to them that we're not a banana republic, that English law will protect their investments,' Steve said assertively. 'We need to find evidence that Sharkey bribed councillors to buy that *first* freehold. Can you do some back-peddling and work through council papers and committee minutes dating back to when Sharkey bought that first freehold in Walker Square. Let's see who the players were at that time. My money is on the Mayor, Mickey Cavandish and Joe Sharkey, our main man's uncle.'

'Will do Steve.'

'Talking about players Sanj, at least one Liverpool institution is keeping the city's stature alive and kicking. I've got two VIP tickets for the Liverpool - Atlético Madrid game at Anfield. Want to join me?'

'Sure, I'll come Steve, thanks. I'll bring my Atlético scarf. Just like Everton, Atlético is the People's Club of their city. Their supporters' fever will spread across the city, you'll see. Bet Liverpool loses.'

Forty-Two

The second week of March 2020

Vanessa Chan, now going by the alias of Julie Ma, felt it her patriotic duty to keep track of developments in the great People's Republic of China. Even though she'd grown up in Hong Kong, and had a British passport, Vanessa identified much more with Beijing. As a kid she'd hated the hypocrisy of the ruling British authorities and resented the privileges of the rich Hong Kong elite living off the profits of tax evasion and international banking, pushing up housing prices so high that only the extremely wealthy could survive with dignity. She grew up knowing in her heart-of-hearts that the Chinese Communist Party would redress this outrageous inequality as they took back control, piece-by-piece.

Vanessa's news source was the China *People's Daily*. She also regularly tuned into CCTV news.

By early-January 2020 she'd learned about the terrible epidemic that was bringing her mother country to an abrupt standstill. Coronavirus, they called it and *lockdown* was the solution.

The worst-affected area was Wuhan, in the Hubei province. Luckily her Uncle Benny Zhang was safe in Beijing.

It was clear to her that this was the result of a western plot to massively destabilise her mother country. Her view was unambiguous: during the global Military Games which took place in the city of Wuhan in the autumn of last year, America's Central Intelligence Agency, with logistical support from British operatives in Hong Kong, had introduced a particularly contagious strain of coronavirus inside the wet market in the centre of the city, setting off an epidemic of unprecedented proportions in the city and elsewhere.

It was no fault of the People's Republic. On the contrary, Vanessa knew that the Party authorities would guide her people through this upheaval like no other country on earth. It would take time and a momentous effort by her people. But only China would truly succeed because only the Chinese people were sufficiently disciplined to win this battle of battles. Freedom was the prize for the winners. Enslavement for the losers.

All in all this *new normal* created the perfect conditions for her and Uncle Benny to launch their fatal plan.

Forty-Three

Wednesday March 22, 2020, VIP Lounge, Anfield stadium, Liverpool FC vs Atlético Madrid FC

'I told you your team would lose Steve.'

'Keep your voice down Sanj. And take that scarf off too'

'No worries, Steve, just tell your red mates I'm a European copper colleague, a Spaniard of Moroccan descent, so I'll keep my Madrid scarf on, thank you very much. OK, amigo. Got to say, Atlético tactics were perfect.'

'If you call defending deep for the whole match then scoring on their three counterattacks perfect, then yes, the best tactics won, and football lost.'

'Sour grapes Steve.'

'At least our team is in Europe pretty much every year. More than you can say for your unsweetened toffees.'

'Now, now. Don't get personal. You know the one thing I like about Liverpool FC is your anthem. *You'll Never Walk Alone.* It's a great tune with great words. What most people don't know is that Liverpool band Gerry and the Pacemakers' version in 1963 was not the first one, was it.'

'Thanks for the history lesson, mate, but…'

'It's an American show tune! Rogers and Hammerstein. From the musical Carousel. Nothing to do with football at all.'

'So what? Can we change the subject?'

'Corona?'

'Yep, I'll have one. Love Mexican beer Sanj. Mine's with lime and a touch of salt.'

'No, Steve, I'm talking Coronavirus. Covid, or whatever else it's called. Bat flu?'

'Oh, that business. Sure. It's a bit like the bog-standard winter flu, only less contagious. All this talk about locking people in their homes like they did in China, it's nonsense. Do you know what my old Mum's gone and done? She's ordered herself a full-length burka. No kidding. She says that wearing a burka nobody will see the vulnerable old lady who's supposed to stay at home and not visit the shops. Can't say I blame her.'

'Mr.s Whittley in a burka. What a sight! Give her my best.'

'Seriously though Sanj. My spies at HQ tell me the police will have to enforce a curfew soon. Lockdown, they call it. Just like in China. I just can't see it coming to that. The British public will never accept it. We're a free country and we'll remain free. I'm against any form of lockdown myself.'

'What if that's the only way we'll be able to stop this virus? Worked well in China. Are you saying we're better than them? You've got to give them credit for that?' Sanjay replied.

'The only credit I give them is for letting it leak out of that virology laboratory in Wuhan.'

'Some of my more left-wing colleagues at the *Post* believe that the CIA planted it inside the wet market there.'

'And you think that Sanj?'

'I'm a journalist and you're a police officer. Peas from the same pod Steve. We know never to believe anything until we put it into print. Then it's God's truth.'

'You'd have made a good police officer you know?'

'Sure. With all that institutionalised racism in the force, I wouldn't have gotten very far. Either that or I'd have been promoted for the wrong reasons. At least in journalism, my words count and readership can't be faked.'

'Oh, I dunno Sanj. With all that fake news now on Facebook?'

'You're right Steve. It's bad news for us old-fashioned print folk. Anyhow, looks like most people have left the stadium now. Time to put away my Atlético scarf, ha! Fish and chips on the way home Steve? Just like old times?'

'Sure. It'll remind me of the days when the *Liverpool Post* served a purpose.'

'Oh yes, tell me oh wise one.'

'When they still wrapped the food up in the day's *Post*.'

'You'll certainly be walking alone if your jokes don't improve. I'll have mine with mushy peas, DI Whittley, and it's your turn to pay.'

Forty-Four

Midnight British time, 7 am Beijing time, March 16, 2020

'Good morning my dear Uncle.'

Vanessa was on her monthly WeChat call with her Uncle Benny.

'Hello, my one and only favourite niece, Vanessa, or should I say Julie Ma? Shouldn't you be in bed by now in your cosy Liverpool flat? I was just watching the match. Liverpool lost! You see, I told you, Manchester United will always be the greatest Premier League team.'

'Uncle Benny. I have a plan. And I need to get your approval.'

'Continue.'

'I believe that we can now speed up procedures. Covid will arrive here in a couple of weeks, maybe earlier. Tonight's match will surely be a super spreader. The UK government, unlike our government in China, will simply not be able to cope with the effects of the pandemic. I predict many, many deaths as well as a lot of chaos as British people will most definitely *not* respect the lockdowns to come. They just don't have the self-discipline we have back home. It will be mayhem over here.'

'Our friend Mr. Luke Sharkey has a pre-existing condition. Asthma, right?'

'Correct Uncle. I think you're understanding where I'm coming from.'

'I do indeed. Better be very careful in the execution of the plan. Use Jenny as much as you want. Money's no object. As you know, she's good. Excellent background and training from the People's Liberation Army before she went private, She has a great track record working for the *crème-de-la-crème* in China since then.'

'Will do Uncle. All is well with you?'

'All good, thanks. Always got to be careful, though. Keeping my head down in most places, and looking up where I need to. You know how it is. Take care my dearest.'

As she pressed the red stop button on her mobile, a message came in on her WeChat app. It was from Jenny Wang.

Got your voice message Julie. Yes, I believe the plan will work. Give me some time. I need to procure the right ingredients and figure out the best concentrate of R needed for it to be fatal without arousing too much suspicion. Let's catch up next week. Usual place, usual time.

Forty-Five

Monday morning, March 23, 2020

Finishing his breakfast, Sanjay heard his phone beep. It was a text from his editor-in-chief. For once her message was short and to the point: *Don't come to the office! Work from home until further notice!*

Covid had officially hit the country and the word *lockdown* was on everyone's lips.

Sanjay was not too worried. He wasn't part of any vulnerable group, though he was a little worried for his parents back in India. Fortunately, he did not have any pre-existing conditions, unlike some of the worn-out hacks at the *Post*. The whole thing will be over by the summer in any case, so why worry? Time to honour all those new year's resolutions. Get fitter. A regular morning run along the river? A whisky-free month? Write that novel? The options were endless.

Sanjay loved to socialise but working from home for a while wouldn't be a problem. Sometimes the office gossip, combined with other people's stress, could make him more tense and nervous. The newspaper's finances were, unlike many, relatively solid. The *Post* had adapted well to the online world and social media. Which reminded Sanjay that he needed to spend some time building up a stronger profile on Twitter and Instagram. Lockdown, or whatever the term was, would surely help him focus more on his own career and self-promotion.

Or maybe he'd finally find love? Romance had been a case of *once bitten twice shy* for Sanjay. When he was in his twenties, Samantha, a film studies major he'd met at Liverpool University, had left him for an older man, a successful American screenwriter, who'd whisked her off to California, leaving him devasted. He'd never fully regained his confidence with women since that painful time.

Not too far from Sanjay's apartment in the city centre, Luke Sharkey was also contemplating his options. He'd installed both Microsoft Teams and a new app called Zoom on his PC in anticipation of lockdown. Graham Backland from Expert Invest had been given some advance warning of the severity of the situation from some of his investors in both Beijing and Hong Kong and had warned his brother Andy. Andy Backland was sitting in the office with Sharkey, and they were testing the software with Uncle Joe Sharkey, who was at home with Sharkey's mother, Mary, at her house in Wavertree.

It took Uncle Joe and Mary five attempts before they established a video line. This was not their thing! They'd managed to get their faces on screen, but only the top halves were visible, and the audio was not functioning. After attempt number seven, Sharkey and Backland said they'd try again later and got down to some more serious business talk.

Sharkey was excited about the Covid pandemic. OK, he had asthma. And yep, it's a respiratory disease. But he wasn't yet forty, so he'd be fine.

The real issue was, how can we benefit from Covid? His first question to Backland was whether it was illegal for his property management company City Hygge to tell investors that due to Covid the Liverpool rental market had dried up, even if it hadn't?

Backland confirmed that it was indeed totally illegal. Worse, if City Hygge rented the apartments out without forwarding the income to the investors, he could be sued for criminal activity.

Shame, thought Sharkey. Backland's beginning to go soft on me.

Moving on to question two, Sharkey reminded Backland of the discussion they'd had on the train back from London when they'd first met with Expert Invest.

'You remember,' he said, 'that master, fail-safe business plan whereby I liquidate one of my companies, then sell the freehold to another of my companies. Still legal?'

Sharkey's gut told him this was the perfect time to do this for his Walker Square development company. Sure, he had a legal requirement to offer the freehold for the investors, as they had first right of refusal. But he knew they wouldn't buy. They didn't even have each other's contact details to coordinate the purchase. Divide and rule. Works every time. Oh, the beauty of this *fractional financing* business model, thought Sharkey. I have them by the short and curlies, don't I?

'Yes, still legal Luke.'

'And what was the next step in our plan, Andy?'

'Once we've sold the freehold to Sharkey International, we cash in a few million quid and call it a Director's loan. It's all legal, Luke. And please don't forget your loyal and faithful lawyer. His cash flow needs a boost as well.'

'I'm drowning in tears, Andy. Then what?'

'We transfer the cash immediately to our Panama offshore accounts and you move the Walker Square development company into *voluntary liquidation*. Your creditors will then have no assets to claim on when they sue you to recuperate their *assured return*, which you never paid them in the first place. All legal and above-board, Luke.'

'What are you waiting for? Start drawing up those papers immediately, Andy!'

Just a few hundred metres away from the office where Sharkey and Backland were plotting their scam, DCI McCartney had gathered his full team at the Merseyside Police HQ for an urgent briefing.

McCartney was wearing a face mask. He explained to his troops that he was the lucky one. That he'd managed to find himself a small stock of face masks at the hospital, but that the situation would get a lot worse before it got better. He had to repeat himself a couple of times as he'd evidently underestimated the problems of speaking clearly through his grade A surgical mask.

In McCartney's view, Liverpool was heading for a Covid Armageddon. There would be fighting in the streets, he said, something which most of his team thought normal, especially on weekend nights. More worryingly, McCartney had seen a statistical analysis predicting that the city's hospital would soon be overloaded with a surge in Covid infections requiring emergency treatment.

The old hospital was still in service as the new hospital was still not open. While the new hospital had plenty of breathing ventilators for patients, the machinery could not be moved to the old hospital due to lack of space. The city council accountants were still not allowing them to open the new hospital, even in a case of a global pandemic, because they were in litigation with Carroll Inc., the builders, who had gone bankrupt. What bureaucratic nonsense!

McCartney explained he'd be working mainly from home, as would many others, with only one-third of HQ officers permitted to be physically present in the building at any one time.

As he spoke, Jane Wilson was texting the suspended Steve Whittley to explain that lockdown should allow her to get better access to the servers in the building, with fewer people around. She suggested they meet every Wednesday morning at nine at the Pier Head for updates.

She was optimistic. She'd already dug out some interesting new stuff on Luke Sharkey.

Forty-Six

Mid-June 2020

Since Covid hit the country, Sanjay had managed to find fodder for his articles to be published most days. His biggest worry was the sharp decrease in crime in the city. Not good for crime reporters like him! At the height of lockdown number one, Sanjay had diversified, writing a weekly piece focusing on the silent streets of Liverpool and the social impacts of lockdown, complete with eerily poignant photos of deserted buildings, alleyways, and shopping malls. *Post* readers loved the series and had asked for more.

It was now late spring and the first lockdown in the country had been eased, but there didn't seem to be any consistency in government policy. One day Sanjay had to stay at home. The next he was back in the office. Then back home again. So he'd just started doing pretty much whatever he wanted, whenever.

In the first week of June Luke Sharkey had announced that he'd put one of his many property development companies, Walker Square Developments, into liquidation. Naturally, this had given Sanjay a whole new boost to the Sharkey saga.

Having spent two weeks researching all the speculative angles to this liquidation, that morning in mid-June Sanjay was putting the finishing touches to one of the most important articles he'd ever written for the *Liverpool Post*.

He loved his headline, *From Hero to Zero*. Normally the headlines were drawn up by specialists, but this time Sanjay had come up with it himself, and his editor was thrilled. The piece was going to be the front-page lead, flowing into pages two and three. Sanjay had cross-checked everything with the legal team and had even asked his mate Steve Whittley to give it a thorough read before publication. This was not allowed by the *Post*, but Sanjay had figured his editor wouldn't find out and Steve knew how to keep mum.

Walker Square was not the first Sharkey company to go bust. One of his developments in another northern city financed on the same fractional model had gone into administration a few months back, before the building was finished, leaving investors to manage the fallout.

Walker Square Developments owed millions to its creditors but had no money left on the balance sheet. Another of his companies was now the outright owner of Prince's Place, a 232-unit riverside residence worth fifty million. But his Walker Square investors could not claim on this, as it was a different legal entity.

Sanjay's research also showed that Expert Invest had also gone bankrupt. Its founder and former director, Graham Backland, had retired and moved to Mauritius, where he'd negotiated a tax-free status for the first ten years of residence.

To complicate matters, the architect that Sharkey used for most of his developments had been struck off the register for dishonesty. He certified the buildings before they were complete, so the building termination certificates were no longer valid. This, combined with the cladding, which the fire authorities said needed replacing, meant that the value of the apartments has gone down massively. All-in-all there must be a lot of angry people out there after Sharkey's head, some of them rich and powerful, Sanjay concluded.

In his ten years at the top of the property market in Liverpool, Sharkey had made a lot of enemies. Maybe some would even want him dead, who knows?

Sanjay had to get to the bottom of this. Knowing how Sharkey operated, there was more, so much more to discover. He needed to dig deeper.

PART THREE
FROM NOVEMBER 16 TO DECEMBER 13, 2020

Forty-Seven

THREE DAYS AFTER THE DEATH OF LUKE SHARKEY
1 am, Monday, November 16, 2020

'Then again,' Steve said, 'there's another possibility in all this mess. Sharkey could have just died from Covid. Simple as that. Period, as our American cousins say.'

'No, Steve. Don't give up. He was murdered. My gut tells me.'

'And my gut tells me I need to get back home soon. Past midnight already. Time goes fast when you're talking murder. Doesn't it just warm your heart that our great city of Liverpool has the rare privilege of being the first city in the country to be placed in Tier Three lockdown?'

'Stay just a few more minutes, no balls. The cops won't be out there, and you know them all in any case. Let's just backtrack. One, we think that Sharkey could have been killed. Two, we don't think anybody killed Sharkey alone. Three, if this is the work of a group of people, how did they do it and who's their leader?

'Thirty minutes max, Sanj. Then I'm out of here.'

'OK, thanks pal.'

Steve began his train of thought. 'Let's talk suspects and motives. Suspect number one, Lania Sharkey. Motive? Life insurance and possible inheritance, but we don't know that for sure. Suspect number 2, Diane Ramsay. Motive? To be with Lania and to benefit from the wealth Lania gets with Sharkey dead. Suspect number 3, Tom Wood, Motive? Sharkey knows too much about his illegal activities at Frankie's and has been blackmailing him. Anyone else you came across in your research? What about Sharkey's sleeping business partner, Mr. Zhang, from Beijing?'

'I found that out from Companies House, where he's recorded as a joint director of Sharkey International, the outfit which now appears to own all his Liverpool freeholds. Sharkey's former personal assistant, who was sacked for no apparent reason, said that Mr. Zhang had a female lawyer working for him, based in London.'

'Exactly, Sanj. I'll get Jane to find out more about Zhang and co. Since lockdown' Jane's been working mainly from home. The force has equipped her with the whole IT works - a high-powered server, fibre-optic mega-speed wifi, not to mention three separate screens in her home office. She's got unlimited access to the servers at HQ, which will come in handy. Says I can visit whenever - discreetly that is, just like I'm here now with you. Family and friend Covid *bubbles* and all that. You know the score.'

'Without Jane, we'll never solve this, will we Steve?'

'She's gold dust. The best, Sanj. You should get closer to her as well.'

'I'll call her, next week.'

'OK, got to go back to my little family bubble now. Joanna will be waiting up for me. Goodnight pal.'

Steve let himself out while Sanjay poured himself a final wee drop of that silky, smooth *Aberlour* Scottish single malt.

Life could be worse, he thought, sipping it slowly. Got to be grateful for small mercies. All those oldies and vulnerable people dropping like flies. So sad and tragic. The Covid lottery. *Xièxiè* China! He was glad his parents were back in India where Covid seemed to be under control, at least for the moment.

Sanjay was beginning to reflect more on karma and reincarnation. He wondered what reincarnated creature Luke Sharkey would be? Most certainly a reptile. A snake maybe? No, more like a crocodile.

With the whisky hitting, Sanjay took his pen and wrote a little ditty, which he read out loud to himself.

Luke Sharkey, what fascination
Inspires and drives my imagination
Many people think you're a crook
And you are, at least in my book
Who did kill you? The jury's out
We'll do our job and clear the doubt
But who'll inspire me, now you're gone?
Rest in peace, you strange, weird one

Reading it out loud again, he decided he'd better stick to prose.

Forty-Eight

Wednesday 1 pm, November 18, 2020, Pier Head, Liverpool

Steve Whittley and Jane Wilson had been meeting every week since lockdown at the Pier Head, close to the Liver Building. On occasion they would take the ferry across the River Mersey to Birkenhead. Most of the essential passenger ferry services had continued to operate during lockdown, with the obvious requirement to be socially distant and wear face masks.

Despite the cold wind, Jane and Steve decided to take the ferry today, staying outside on the deck for a more private discussion. They then took a short walk in Birkenhead and came back on the return ferry.

Jane's briefing focused on what she'd garnered on Facebook. Her fake alias as an owner/resident of Walker Square had been accepted by the Admins of both the resident and investor Facebook pages. The page Admins had been somewhat lax in letting people into the group. Jane said that the ease with which she entered the group led her to believe that Luke Sharkey had trolls on these same pages.

She'd succeeded in luring some of them with some clickbait. And guess what? All the troll links led back one person: Luke Sharkey. He wasn't that digitally savvy, as he'd left traces all over the place. Unfortunately, Jane was unable to find anything that compromised Sharkey, criminally speaking, that is.

She then explained to Steve that there were two persons on both the resident and investor Facebook sites that she could *not* identify, nor place anywhere else on the web, Jenny W and Julie M. In contrast to Sharkey, these two were digital natives and experts. Through cross-referencing she'd figured they were neither owners nor residents in any of Sharkey's developments. So why would they be on these sites and who were they?

Other names that came up on both Facebook sites included Tom Wood and Diane Ramsay and Lania Sharkey. From their frequent digital correspondence on Facebook Messenger, it was clear that Diane was a very close and intimate friend of Lania Sharkey.

Explaining all this digital stuff to Steve, Jane quickly twigged that he was not a digital native. He wasn't even on Facebook. Understandable, she thought, given his present situation. Nevertheless, she wondered how anyone could survive and prosper in the twenty twenties without Facebook? Jane had become a social media junkie, to such an extent that her partner Crys had recently forced her to get some psychological help, as it was beginning to negatively impact their marriage.

Finishing her update Jane said, 'And get this, Steve. Yesterday, Diane Ramsay called the police to report a break-in at her flat in Walker Square. We sent someone around to investigate, but she decided to withdraw her complaint. Very strange and quite uncommon, don't you think Steve?'

'It certainly is, Jane. Perhaps she's hiding something?'

Back on shore Steve thanked Jane once again and said that he'd gladly accept her invitation for a discreet, and illegal lockdown dinner at her home to inspect her glitzy new IT set-up. Not that he'd understand much about the technology, apart from the fact that it was costing the force a lot of money they probably couldn't afford.

They fixed the date and went their separate ways, keeping their facemasks on as extra protection against the stinging, cold horizontal rain that was beginning to come in from the Irish Sea.

Forty-Nine

Wednesday mid-morning, November 25, 2020

By now, Steve, Jane and Sanjay were convinced that Luke Sharkey had been murdered. Their prime suspect was now Tom Wood. Again, they needed more evidence. Jane's intel was that there might be an incriminating video on Tom's mobile phone. To get hold of this, she'd concocted a plan to *borrow* Wood's phone without him noticing. To do this, they'd need to make a surprise visit to Frankie's.

By coincidence, Steve's brother Nick and his partner Witold knew Tom Wood quite well. A few years ago when Tom had opened Frankie's nightclub, they'd been regular clients. Back then it was a pleasant, gay-friendly live music club without being 'overly' gay, which suited them well. For several years, it had been their favourite weekend hangout.

Since Tom had started employing his male and female *students*, Nick and Witold had stopped going, disgusted by the new set-up. They'd even reported these abuses to Steve, who'd passed the information on to the relevant police department.

Frankie's was presently closed due to lockdown, but Wood had been illegally opening it to a small group of his wealthier and more influential punters, for a bumped-up entry fee of course. Jane's plan was for Nick and Witold to go to the club like old friends and distract Tom, while Steve somehow got into his office to find whatever evidence he could regarding Luke Sharkey's suspicious death, including his mobile phone. Steve would pretend to be Nick if he was seen.

For the plan to work, Steve and Nick needed to look *exactly* the same again, for the first time since they were teenagers, but the twins' different hairstyles and dress codes these days made them easily distinguishable. Which meant one thing: a visit to their barber on Penny Lane!

Steve called Nick, asking him to meet him on the corner of Penny Lane at midday. He explained that their barber had agreed to open the shop discreetly, with the blinds down; his tattoo artist friend would also be there.

On the phone Nick was reluctant, saying that there must be a reason that the government had banned all non-essential shops from opening, and the reason was to stop the spread of a deadly disease, uh! He also said that he didn't need a haircut.

'I understand, Nick,' Steve said, 'but there is an even better reason that we need you to come. I need you to pretend to be me, and me to pretend to be you.'

'That's not going to work bro.'

'Hold on. Let me explain further. Jane, Sanjay and I are working on a murder case. It happened just two weeks ago. We need evidence. And we can only get this with your help.'

'How come you're working on a case when you're still suspended?'

'It's complicated, Nick, but stay with me. If we solve this one, then the chances are I'll be reinstated. Can't give you any more details about the victim, but I can explain how you and Witold are going to help us.'

'Witold? Don't bring him into it, please.'

'We've already spoken to him and he's up for it.'

'Behind my back? That's how you lot work, is it? Not nice.'

'He wants to help Nick. Especially when I told him the name of our suspect - Tom Wood.'

'Tom Wood. Manager at Frankie's. That bastard pimp. Escort boys, mainly from eastern Europe, that's his business now. Well, men legally speaking, as they're over eighteen years old, but they all look younger.

'Actually Nick, you could call it a co-ed establishment nowadays. He calls them his *students*, as a lot of them aspire to further education in the UK once they've made the money and got their residence papers. Modern slavery, I'm sad to say.'

'And you lot should be doing more to stop this. What a disgusting man!'

'We try, Nick. But there are so many legal loopholes, and Tom Wood knows them all.'

As the conversation progressed, Nick was changing his mind.

'OK Steve, I'm up for it, together with Witold. We cannot let dirt like Tom Wood continue this abuse, never mind what you suspect him to have done. Murderer? Tom Wood? Oh my God.'

'Thanks Nick. Much appreciated. As I said, for the plan to work, we've got to look *exactly* the same, just like we were when we were born, bro.'

'I'll meet you at the barber's at twelve,' Nick said, 'as long as you accept just one condition.'

'I agree,' Steve said, without asking what the condition was, ready to take any fraternal deal at this point.

'You must adapt to *my* look, not me to yours. My hairstyle, my clothes, my tattoos. I'm the original. After all, you are my younger brother. Get it?'

'Get it,' Steve replied, affirmatively.

Jane spent the next few minutes explaining all the details of her plan. All three would need to gain entrance to Frankie's via the outside fire escape, which was now being used by Tom's illegal guests instead of the more visible front door on the main street. With Steve hiding in the background, Nick and Witold would ask the security guard to call Tom to let them in, for old times' sake.

What could possibly go wrong?

Fifty

Wednesday midday, November 25, 2020, Penny Lane Barber Shop, Liverpool

Steve was pleased his brother was in. He was less happy about now having to adopt Nick's somewhat bohemian style. This meant taking his dyed black back to a natural grey colour, which was quite a challenge for their barber, who gave them trendy and younger cuts, with a grey mop on top, and closely shaven sides.

Next came the addition of a temporary copy of Nick's arm tattoo. Steve had never paid much attention to Nick's tattoos. He had them all over his body, but the only one visible with a short-sleeved shirt was on his arm. This had to be replicated on Steve's arm. It was made up of text in black, *Love My Hun*, inside a big, fading red heart, with an arrow through it.

'Never noticed that one Nick. So corny.'

'It's a play on words. Witold also has a tattoo on his arm. *Love my island ape*. Get it?'

'I get the Hun bit. Short for honey, no doubt. Joanna wouldn't mind me having that one, if I explained it right. She may even ask me to make it permanent,' Steve said. 'I don't understand Witold's *island ape*, though.'

'Germans call us Brits *island apes*, apparently. I thought it was funny, which is why I had my Hun tattoo. Get it now bro?'

'Don't mention the war, and all that?'

'Yeah, funny, eh?'

'If you say so.'

When all the work was done Steve gave an extra big tip to the barber and his tattoo artist colleague. After all, he'd illegally opened his shop by the back door and could have been nicked.

Nick had arrived in a taxi, so they took Steve's car back for lunch in Crosby, where Nick and Witold owned a beautiful house overlooking Liverpool Bay, the entrance to the River Mersey. As they approached Crosby beach, they reminisced about how strong swimmers they were when they were teenagers, having been Saturday regulars at the old Wavertree pool. They'd both swum for the school team and could have competed at county level. Then Steve discovered cricket and Nick music, and that was that.

Along the sea road they passed the famous Gormely statue on the beach.

In the late nineties, Antony Gormely, a well-known British artist, had forged one-hundred-cast replicas of his own body. These had been exhibited in different countries across Europe before being permanently concreted into the sand at strategic spots over a two-mile stretch on Crosby beach.

Each figure measures six feet in height, and all are visible at low tide. As the tide comes in, the statues are gradually submerged until all one hundred are covered by water at high tide.

The statues are a big attraction; locals regularly dressed them up in Liverpool and Everton football gear and other less flattering attire.

'Nick, bet I'd beat you swimming out to the furthest statue. On for a race next summer?'

'You must be kidding Steve. Swimming on Crosby beach? Suicide mission bro. With all those crazy currents and that fast, incoming tide. No way.'

'Chicken. You're getting soft and you're aging twice as fast as your younger, more handsome twin. I'm up for it, if ever you change your mind.'

'That will not happen.'

Fifty-One

Friday evening, November 27, 2020, Frankie's Night Club, Liverpool City Centre

Jane dropped off Witold, Nick and Steve at the back of Frankie's nightclub at around 10.30 pm. Nick and Steve were dressed the same, right down to their black socks and shoes. They'd remained pretty much the same weight as each other over the years; Steve tended to drink more, and Nick eat more, equalising out the weight gain.

The exterior temperature was above zero. It rarely fell below zero degrees Celsius in Liverpool, even at the height of winter. Witold loved Nick, loved his job, loved Liverpool, but he hated the weather in that part of England. By now he'd spent more of his adult life there than in Munich, but he still hadn't figured out how to dress for the Liverpool weather. Maybe the clue was to dress each day for *all* seasons. The humidity made him sweat, even when it was cold outside, and once inside he always had to remove layers of clothing to cool back down to a normal, European body temperature.

When he was a kid Witold used to watch Inspector Derrick, a popular German TV detective series. Looking up at the fire escape stairs in anticipation at the night's escapade, he fancied himself as a modern-day, younger, and more handsome Derrick, but without his pistol. This was murky work. Murkier than the River Mersey, he thought, if that is possible.

From what Steve and Jane had told him and Nick at the briefing earlier, the whole property development scene in Liverpool had become intermingled with local politics to produce an ugly powder keg of corruption ready to explode at any moment. Tonight, Witold was going to do his small bit for justice in this city. How exciting.

They climbed up the metal fire escape to the third-floor door that had the sign Exit Only above a peephole that could only be opened from the inside. Nick and Witold rang the bell while Steve remained out of sight, a few steps down. The door was opened, but only as far as the chain would allow.

'Names please.'

'Nick and Witold. Tell Tom we're here and we'd love to buy him a drink and catch up. For old times' sake. He'll understand.'

The door was closed and all three remained outside for what seemed like an eternity.

'OK, come on in, the heavy-set bouncer said, opening the door wide.

As Nick and Witold walked in, Nick put his arm around the doorman and gave him a big kiss on the cheek.

'Hi there, Jay. It's been a long time. You're looking great.'

The doorman was distracted both by Nick's affectionate kiss and his gentle, but firm arm around him.

While this was happening, Witold gave Steve the sign. The ruse worked to perfection, Steve slipping into the club without the security guard noticing.

'Nice greeting gentlemen, but I'm not Jay. He left before Covid and is still lying low. He's got diabetes and has been on a self-imposed house lockdown for months. Can't say I blame him.'

'Sorry, mate. Just that you look a bit like him, only better.'

'Yeah, sure. Flattery, and all that. Strange. I must be getting old. I'm sure I saw another person come in just now, spitting image of you in fact.'

'Na. You're dreaming. Have you had a Covid PCR check recently? Hallucination is one of the symptoms. Didn't you know that? Drink later?'

Steady on Nick, thought Witold, don't lay it on too thick!

'I can't, pal. Never on duty. And my name's Jamie. Not too far from Jay, eh? Have a good night, friends. See you later.'

Nick had drawn Steve a map of the interior, which Steve had memorised. Inside the club, Steve headed for the back of the small stage that used to host live bands and comedians, before Tom took the establishment downhill into escort territory. Most of the time the curtain was closed, as it was tonight, providing cover from where Steve could hear conversations from the bar area.

Glancing to his right on his way to the stage, Steve had seen Mayor Ferguson, Councilman Joe Sharkey, City Regeneration Head Mickey Cavandish, and surprise, surprise, Andy Backland, Luke Sharkey's lawyer. They were sipping whisky and coke at the same table and laughing. Could you believe it? Liverpool had been the first English city to go into the strictest, central-government-imposed Covid Tier Three regulations, and this club was hosting the Mayor leading his cronies in a drunken fest, with no face masks in sight.

Earlier that week Sanjay had told Steve this was happening all over the city. Always the cop, Steve never fully believed other people's stories until he saw the evidence first-hand. And now there was no doubt: Sanjay's sources were right.

Nick and Witold had been warmly welcomed by Tom Wood at the bar. This was going to be tricky for them, as they'd both come to despise the man.

'Been a while. You're not looking a day older, gentlemen. The usual?' Tom had an amazing memory for his customers' drinks - gin and tonic for Nick and a Singapore Sling for Witold.

Tom's office was behind the bar. The only access from the interior of the club to the office was via the bar. The office has a second door connected to the fire escape. That outside door, though, would certainly be locked, so Steve needed to move through the bar to get to Tom's office.

They needed a distraction, so they'd planned in advance to ask Tom to give them a short tour of the club, which had changed a lot since they'd last been there.

They'd already agreed that the all-clear sign to Steve would be a ringtone on Witold's phone to the tune of *You'll Never Walk Alone*. All Nick had to do was to reach into his pocket and press the call button to Witold, launching *You'll Never Walk Alone*.

Sipping their drinks at the bar together, Tom seemed genuinely pleased to see Nick and Witold. They spent some time talking about the past and how everything was so much better back then. Tom explained that many of his regulars like them had got older and more settled and gradually stopped coming. Even though he regretted it, the only way to keep the income flowing was to bring in the *students*. Yes, he was sorry. But no, he had to make a living somehow and he assured Nick and Witold that his *students* were well-treated, benefited from top-class Sharkey Group accommodation in Walker Square, were well paid and worked no more than four nights per week.

Of course, he didn't tell them he retained all of their passports and other important documents in a locked safe in his back office.

Suddenly Witold's phone began to ring to the tune of *You'll Never Walk Alone*. Shit! Witold had completely forgotten. He'd also programmed that tune for his mother, back in Munich, who often called him late at night when she couldn't sleep. Thinking fast, and already on his feet, Witold grabbed his chest with both hands. Just before he spoke, he gave a big eye wink to Nick.

'I'm not feeling well Nick.'

Witold fell onto the floor, clutching his chest. Nick had understood the sign. Witold was faking a heart attack. Nick immediately asked Tom if he could use his phone to call an ambulance, explaining that Witold had recently been diagnosed with a serious heart condition.

Nick watched closely as Tom opened his phone, memorising the six-digit code Tom had tapped in. Having then given Nick his phone to call the ambulance, Tom ran across the room, getting Jamie to close the place urgently and move the punters out quickly, including Mayor Ferguson and his drunken cronies.

Steve slipped into Tom's office and Nick used the five minutes Tom was away to exchange the phone passwords. As luck would have it, Tom had owned the same mobile phone brand and version as he did, so the changes were easy. Nick then pocketed Tom's phone and left his own on the bar, with the code duly readjusted, for Tom to take when he returned.

'Quick thinking Hun. But promise me, don't ever do this again,' Nick whispered to Witold, playing dead on the floor.

'Didn't you get the sign when I winked? Couldn't have been more obvious, no?'

'I did, Witold, I did, straightaway. You still gave me a shock. Guess that's why you teach drama at school. Hang on in there while I now will give you some fake CPR. I'll promise not to be too rough.'

'I've heard that before,' Witold replied. 'Get going then.'

It took seven minutes for Jamie and Tom to escort all the customers down the outside fire escape as the medics rushed up the inside staircase. Arriving at the bar, the medics put Witold on a stretcher and fixed him up with some oxygen. After fifteen minutes of tests, they explained to Nick that Witold seemed to have made an amazingly quick recovery, and that all the numbers were back to normal, as if nothing had ever happened.

Still acting as though his life depended on it, Witold stood up, helped by Nick. He thanked the medical staff for their vigilance and support and insisted that he'd be alright from now on, that there was no need for him to spend the night at the hospital.

By this time Tom had picked up what he thought to be his own mobile phone on the bar and put it into his jacket pocket. Moving behind the bar, he served himself a large whisky and took it into his back office, where Steve was now hiding, under a very old, shabby-chic Victorian desk. He went over to his safe and opened it to put the evening's cash takings in.

Rushing back out of the office in a rage, Tom shouted to his barman 'What have you done with the passports, you little shitbag.'

The young Asian man was stunned and replied that he had not seen nor taken any passports and didn't know what Tom was talking about. Tom insisted and grabbed him by the hair, dragging him to the floor. At this point Nick split the two up and took Tom down to the floor threatening to call the police if he didn't calm down. Tom relented and apologised, and went back into his office, where Steve was still under the Victorian study table.

This gave Nick and Witold some time to plan the next steps to get Steve out safely.

Still acting a little faint, Witold asked Jamie to help him over to a table on the other side of the room where the Mayor and his mates had been seated earlier. Witold asked Jamie to sit with him for a while until he mustered the energy to be on his way.

With Jamie and Witold away from the bar, and Steve still under the table in Tom's office, Nick rushed to the door and made a hasty exit down the fire escape, without anyone seeing him leave. He found a good spot to hide at the bottom of the outside stairs and remained there.

A few minutes later at the table, Witold said he was ready to leave now, and Jamie escorted him to the fire escape door. Witold left and Jamie closed the outside door behind him.

Witold waited five minutes outside the fire escape door then rang the bell. Jamie opened the door immediately, with a worried look on his face.

'Oh, it's you again. Are you ok? Having a relapse? Was afraid it was the cops. I've had enough drama for one night.'

'Sorry, Jamie, I just need one last favour. I need to call Tom. Can I borrow your phone, please?'

'Sure. No problem,' Jamie replied, handing Witold his mobile.

Witold called Tom, who picked up straightaway, still sitting at his desk.

'This is Tom, how can I be of help?'

'It's Witold, Tom. I've lost Nick. And I need him to take me home, quickly.'

'Understand Witold, mate. Hope you're ok. I'll have a look around the club to see if I can find him.'

'Thanks Tom, you're the best.'

With Steve still crouched under his study table, Tom left his office to look for Nick, as Witold had requested. This allowed Steve to sneak back out of Tom's office through the bar area, where he saw Tom opening the stage curtain to see if Nick was there. Steve headed for the toilets. After a fake pee, he came out and was standing face-to-face with Tom.

Tom was relieved. 'So glad to find you Nick. What a night! Witold thought he'd lost you. He's with Jamie at the fire escape door. You'd better be going.'

'Thanks Tom,' Steve said. You've been great. Without your help he could have died. Much appreciated. See you soon mate.'

Fifty-Two

Saturday morning, 3 am, November 28, 2020, Liverpool City Centre

Instead of heading home, Steve, Nick and Witold decided to walk to Sanjay Singh's place, close by. As they were walking Steve texted Sanjay saying that they were on their way, even if it was three o'clock in the morning. What he didn't know was that Jane had already given Sanjay the Heads Up earlier that night, and the two of them were still up, waiting for news.

Ten minutes later, around the coffee table in Sanjay's lounge, Steve recounted the evening's drama. He was angry and pissed off that all they had to show for their trials and tribulations were some useless passports found in the open safe in Tom's office. Not much use in the Luke Sharkey murder inquiry?

Dammit, if only his brother and Witold hadn't messed things up.

'Steve' said Nick, 'you've always underestimated me haven't you. And you know it.'

'Let's not start that bro. We're very different, that's all. Some of us are losers and some of us....'

'Winners,' shouted Nick. 'Ha, I knew you'd rise to the bait. Oh, look what I've found dear brother. A phone. I wonder who that belongs to?'

Nick handed the phone to Jane, who swiped it open. 'Eureka. Tom Wood's mobile. You're a genius Nick.'

'And Witold....'

'He's a genius too.'

Jane, who was sitting next to Steve, opened the phone and started to examine the contents. She opened an app and clicked on a video, which showed Tom Wood and Diane Ramsay at Frankie's examining some open plastic capsules, with some powder spilled out on the bar. Jane did a quick search on the internet. The capsules were asthma medication for inhalers. Very strange.

Fifty-Three

Two days later, Crosby Beach, Liverpool Bay

After the adventure of that Friday night, Witold and Nick spent the weekend relaxing in their beautiful Crosby home.

From the front bay windows, overlooking their small lawn, they had a direct view out into Liverpool Bay. When the tide was high, they could give a thumbs up to the merchant ship captains sailing in to dock their goods at the Bootle container port. They often saw tourists waving from the cruise boats coming in and out of the city from numerous destinations. Earlier that year they'd planned a cruise from Liverpool, around Scotland and over to Scandinavia, taking in the Norwegian fjords, then down the coast and into the Baltic Sea. They'd had to postpone the trip. Thanks again Covid!

Most days they made time to walk Gustav their golden retriever dog on the long sandy beaches, taking in the weird and wonderful sights of the Gormely statues and guessing what attire they'd be dressed up in today.

It was a chilly, windy Sunday afternoon, but the sun was shining, if somewhat low in that autumn sky. Gustav was impatient, but Witold was working on some lessons for the next day at school. Nick said he'd take Gustav out and that Witold should join them when he'd finished. Nick figured this was as good a day as any for a jog, thinking it would help release the pent-up tension in his body after that frantic Friday night. Witold hated running and said he'd meet him later when he went for his walk.

Jogging along the beach with Gustav zigzagging along with him, Nick noticed an uncommon event on these sands. Near one of the Gormely statues, one woman and two men were having some sort of judo or taekwondo session. Or was it Thai boxing? The men looked quite big and stocky, whereas the woman was slighter and a lot smaller. From what he could see, the woman seemed pretty good, and had landed some foot punches on both burly men's faces. For a practice session, he thought, this seemed serious stuff.

Further out, another woman, splashing in the water, appeared to be tied to a Gormely statue located closest to the fast-moving, incoming waters, which were already up to her waist.

Nick was a strong swimmer and a trained lifeguard. But it had been many years since he and Steve had earned their pocket money as supervisors at their local swimming pool. The advice was always to take a floating aid with you when helping someone in distress. The nearest one was on the shore, a good three hundred metres away from where Nick was now. By the time he'd gone there and back the tide would have fully immersed the women tied to the statue. He had no choice.

He undressed quickly to his boxer shorts and ran into the water towards the woman. She was a good fifty meters away and the strong current was taking him south, towards the city. Adjusting for this, he struggled to get closer and closer and made it within arm's reach. He grabbed the statue and began to untie the ropes that strapped the woman to the statue. One knot was so tight that he couldn't untie it. Suddenly, to his right, he saw the same woman who'd been fighting with the two men swimming strongly towards him with what looked like a Swiss army knife tied and flapping around her neck. And next to her, Gustav, his dog, swimming strongly, pulling a floating aid! It was almost surreal!

The fighting woman pulled out the knife and dived to the bottom of the statue. What seemed like an eternity passed, then she resurfaced, explaining to Nick in a local scouse accent that the ropes were all free now. Together, they helped the woman who had been tied up back to the shore, with Gustav leading and Nick taking up the rear. As they were walking out of the water, still fighting the strong current, a small rubber dinghy drew up beside them with DCI McCartney and Jane Wilson on board.

'Whittley,' shouted McCartney, 'you should know better not to risk your life for this. We were on our way here and the other boat's divers are still there looking to see if there are any other persons trapped out there.'

Nick didn't know quite what to do. Looking at Jane's expression, and somehow hearing her unspoken message, he replied 'Sorry, sir, but this was an urgent situation. Had I not got there in time, she'd have drowned. Didn't have time to call the police. Thanks for being there all the same.'

'You're welcome, Steve,' replied McCartney. 'I can see that since you've been on temporary leave you've gone a bit crazy with the tattoos. When you're reinstated, which I hope will be soon, I'll put you on the drugs squad. They all have tattoos. Bet Joanna loves that Hun one.'

'Thank you, sir. Can't wait to be reinstated, but you must solve this Sharkey business first. I'm told Jane is getting closer.'

'She is, Whittley, she is. And we're getting great help for once from the *Liverpool Post*, especially that Sanjay Singh fellow. He seems to know a lot about Sharkey's business dealings. We'll get there soon enough. Good to see you're still up for a few heroics, Steve.'

'Thank you again sir. Glad to be of service.'

A crowd had gathered with towels and protective clothing. Nick, Jane and DCI McCartney turned their attention to the two women, who were both of Chinese ethnicity. But only one remained. The martial arts woman was already quite far in the distance, running as fast as she could back to the beach road. Very strange.

Addressing the woman who had been tied to the statue, the detective chief inspector said 'Hello Ma'am, I'm DCI McCartney. This is PC Jane Wilson. And the brave but stupid man that saved you is DI Steve Whittley, or he was a DI until he was suspended some time ago. And you are?'

'Julie Ma, sir. A law student at Liverpool University.'

'Well, Ms. Ma, I should imagine that you will want to accompany us to the station to issue a formal complaint against those yobs that did this to you, won't you?'

'That's very good of you sir, and I appreciate it, but there's no need. I won't be making any formal complaint. I'm sure it's a case of mistaken identity. I'm often taken for somebody I'm not. Happens to many of my Chinese student friends here.'

'Well, we're very sorry about that and we fully understand. Are you sure that you don't want to? Without a formal complaint we cannot make a charge against the people who roughed you up. Our job is to get the perpetrators. It would be a travesty to justice if we let them get away with this.'

'Honestly, officer, I'm ok and do not need to take this any further.'

'Ok then, it's your choice. Jane, could you look after Ms. Ma and have her driven back to her student digs.'

Julie Ma, alias Vanessa Chan, decided she must accept this offer. Refusing assistance would seem suspicious. Jane escorted her to an awaiting police car and was driven back to her digs Walker Square. Jane returned immediately to McCartney.

Nick was wondering how to get out of twin brother imitation mode, when Gustav started to run down the beach to greet the approaching Witold. Time to get out of here, thought Nick. He quickly explained to McCartney and Jane that he needed to stop Gustav from entering the water again. Wishing them all a very good day, he ran down the beach after Gustav, who had already caught up with Witold.

Back at the scene, DCI McCartney was enjoying his control of proceedings. 'In our work we sure get to see some strange stuff, eh Jane. I'm going to miss the excitement when I retire, you know.'

'And when will that be sir?'

'Soon, Jane. As soon as we've solved this Sharkey business and reinstated Whittley. Maybe he'll take my place as the new DCI? I know you'd like that and so would many others at HQ.'

'I hope so too, sir. As for the victim, Julie Ma, I'll check her profile and digital imprint and write the report asap.'

McCartney didn't reply and was staring into the low western sky.

'Sir?' Jane said.

'Sorry Wilson, I was miles away, dreaming of my cottage in Wales. Can't wait. Or *ni allaf aros*, as they say in those Welsh hills.'

Fifty-Four

Wednesday mid-morning, December 2, 2020, Jane and Crys's house, Sefton, Liverpool

With his face mask fully covering his mouth and nose, Steve surreptitiously looked left, right, and behind him, as if he were breaking into the place, before ringing the bell of Jane and Crys's three-bedroom semi-detached house in Sefton, in south Liverpool. Lockdown had not yet been lifted, so he had to be careful. It seemed like everyone was watching everyone.

Contrary to what many people in the country had assumed at the outbreak of Covid, most Brits had been very law-abiding, and some had even taken a certain sadistic pleasure reporting their neighbours to the police if they so much as welcomed people into their homes not in their personal *bubble.*

Jane opened the door, still in her Japanese satin dressing gown.

'Come on in Steve. Nobody's watching, apart from Mr.s Brown at number thirty-six. She never stops watching, nothing to do with Covid. She's harmless. Crys says hello. She's gone out for a jog. She can't keep a secret and would rather not be around when we're talking business. Doesn't want to get involved. Coffee?'

'That would be lovely, thanks.'

The house was much larger inside than it looked from the outside. It was as deep as it was wide, and the previous owner had put an extension onto the back of the house, eating into the garden. Jane's office was there overlooking a quaint little pond with goldfish, and a small water fountain. Hanging on the wall were some pictures of Jane's mother and father in Hong Kong in the seventies. There was also one of Crys and Jane as well as a collage of photos of Jane in police uniform, including one with Steve's fraternal arms around her at a Christmas party ten years ago.

Jane served coffee and they both sat down at the table.

'Nice photos. You haven't aged one bit, and neither have I,' Steve said, laughing to himself. Jane had always loved Steve's chuckle and his sense of humour. It was catching. He was her favourite boss, the best she'd ever had, and always would be, suspended or not.

156

'Down to business, DI Whittley. Let me explain what I've got, starting with Julie Ma, that unfortunate woman who you saved from drowning. Oh, sorry, it was your brother Nick. Forgot, ha!'

'The worst thing is,' Steve replied, 'I'll have to keep those temporary tattoos because McCartney's already seen them. At least until he retires.'

'Joanna told me she likes them, so why not make them permanent? She is your Hun, isn't she?'

'Looks like I'll have to start calling her that now,' Steve sighed.

'Julie Ma's real name is Vanessa Chan. A British Hong Konger, just like my Mum. She was reprimanded in her youth by the Hong Kong police for disturbance of the peace several times but was never charged. She did her law degree here in Liverpool. Became a member of the Chinese Communist party before we handed back Hong Kong to China in nineteen-ninety-seven, when she was only seventeen years old. That's quite rare, as I'm sure you know, Steve. It appears she hated the British occupation of Hong Kong and seems to have retained that animosity to this day. How can anyone be so naïve, I ask you?'

'Most young students from Hong Kong I've met here hate the new laws there and are fighting valiantly each day for their freedoms. Julie Ma is an exception. I wonder why?'

'Vanessa Chan, Steve, not Julie Ma.'

'Sorry, Jane, I meant Vanessa Chan.'

'Vanessa's uncle, Mr. Benny Zhang, is also a member of the Communist Party of the People's Republic of China. Opportunistic, according to my research. Seems like he's more interested in making a buck or two, or should I say a few billion bucks or two, than being an apparatchik. He's got big property portfolios in Hong Kong, Shanghai, and Beijing. I've not been able to trace anything to England, yet.'

'Her uncle is Benny Zhang? That's interesting. Sanjay mentioned his name to me the other day. He's a co-director of the Sharkey Group, according to Companies House in London. Well, what do you know!'

'Turns out Zhang became a father figure to Vanessa Chan when her parents died in a plane crash in the nineties, and they've been very close ever since.'

'Now I remember. On one of my tours a couple of weeks ago a young woman called Julie Ma asked me a question. She wanted to know who owned the residential developments in the Ropewalks area. I told her a lot of them belonged to the Sharkey Group. I also told her to check out Sanjay's pieces in the *Post*. Why would she be on my tour Jane? And why would she ask me that question?'

'What if she knew you were the lead detective for Operation Croft before being suspended? She was probably checking you out. Was she with anyone else?'

'Yes.'

'This woman?' Jane showed Steve a photo on her phone.

'Yes, I think it was. Yes, that's her alright.'

'She goes by the name of Jenny Wang. At least that's the alias for her stay in Liverpool. Former Chinese People's Liberation Army turned private detective for hire. Nick would certainly recognise her face. She was the woman who helped him save Vanessa Chan from drowning the other day. I think that we can safely assume that there's more to this connection than meets the eye, Steve.'

'You could say that, yes.'

Fifty-Five

Friday 11 pm, December 4, 2020, Frankie's Night Club

Tom Wood had wanted to keep Frankie's closed until the whole situation calmed down. Witnessing Witold's heart attack and having to bribe the ambulance staff not to say anything was a close shave. Better now to lie low.

Trouble was, Mayor Ferguson and his cronies wouldn't take no for an answer. Guess they needed their playtime as well. At the door, Tom had instructed Jamie not to let anyone else in that night, not even Witold and Nick. The Mayor and his gang were at their usual table. Better to keep it all under control tonight. For once, the *less* the merrier, Tom figured.

Jamie was smoking a cigarette outside the fire escape door when he felt a sharp pain in the solar plexus, then a strong, tightening arm around his neck. The next thing he knew he was on his knees on the metal steps, bound and gagged to the railings. This was the first time he'd seen these two women at Frankie's. They'd swiftly taken his phone and his keys, so there was not much else for him to do but sit this one out. What humiliation!

In the dim-lit entryway, no one noticed as Julie Ma and Jenny Wang slipped into the club. With the staff attending to the mayor's table, access through the bar to Tom's office was easy. Tom was sitting, laid back, feet up on his old Victorian desk. His black shoes were shiny on top, but the soles were beginning to wear through on the bottom. Before he knew it, Jenny Wang had tied his legs together and pulled him off his seat, dragging him onto the floor. Vanessa had tied his arms behind his back with plastic strapping and tensioner. Jenny had then gagged him with strong duct tape and together they'd rolled him into the beer-stained, cigarette-burned old rug and stood him upright, with just his head struggling out of the top.

'Nice to see you, Tom. Looking good. Your new suit fits you very well. You must tell me if it's too tight. We can get our tailors to adjust it,' whispered Vanessa, barely disguising her delight seeing Tom so helpless.

Jenny watched the door while Vanessa progressively taunted Tom with insults about his masculinity, before moving on to the crux of the matter.

'Thought you could get me killed, eh. Thought it would be easy, did you? Thought your scumbag scouse heavies would be a match for us little Asian girls, eh? Ha! It's payback time now Tom. Shall we begin down there?' Vanessa pointed to Tom's genitals 'or are they just too small to be worth the effort?'

Tom grunted through his duct tape muffle.

Vanessa then took out a flick knife and pointed it to Tom's cheek.

'OK my friend. I'm going to remove the tape and I want you to remain silent. You will only speak when I say so, understand?'

Vanessa ripped the tape off so violently that Tom's stubble was torn off with it.

'Listen carefully, my friend. Tomorrow morning PC Jane Wilson and DCI McCartney of the Merseyside Police will receive the video of you giving Diane Ramsay the asthma inhaler capsules that killed Luke Sharkey. This is evidence that you *aided and abetted*, and you will go to prison. To be on the safe side, I've also sent a second copy to our journalist friend, Sanjay Singh from the *Post*.'

'What do you mean, the capsules killed Luke Sharkey?' Tom was so desperate, he decided to break Vanessa's imposed silence.

'Did I say you could speak?'

'I want to help, I do. Sharkey died from Covid. Everyone knows that. It was in his obituary in the *Post*.'

'And you believe all you read in the paper, you naïve little western *gweilo*.' Vanessa was enjoying this.

'I'm sorry, but I don't understand the connection between asthma capsules and Sharkey's death?' pleaded Tom.

'You'll find out soon when the police charge you. I think the minimum sentence for *aiding and abetting* in the case of murder is three years. Don't forget, though, you'll get many more years if I spill the beans about the men you hired to try to kill me. My assistant over there is a smart woman. Very smart. She's also a geek and copied your phone records the other day, including the telephone conversations you had when you hired those amateur heavies.'

'You stole my phone, eh? How did you get into the club? Are you paying the doorman?'

Vanessa was bluffing about Jenny copying his phone records, so she was a little taken aback by Tom's reply. Someone else must have stolen his phone, but who? Bad news. How much other evidence was on his mobile that could implicate her and Jenny? Calm, no worries. It'll be ok.

'Yep, that's right. We've been paying Jamie for some time now. We took your phone the other evening.'

'That slimy, two-faced bastard. After all I've done for him over the years. Saved his ass so many times. Ungrateful piece of…'

'Shut up and listen! This is what you're going to do. When the police ask you about me, you will say nothing. Get it Tom? Nothing. If you value your balls, you'd better obey me. Have a nice evening.'

Vanessa and Jenny left the club without anyone seeing them, with Tom still wrapped up in the old carpet in his back office. On their way out they freed Jamie from the fire escape and advised him to start looking for another job. Two hours later, one of Tom's *students,* who had been working the bar and serving the Mayor's group, discovered Tom in the office, eyes closed, face as white as a sheet, mumbling to himself.

Fifty-Six

Saturday morning, December 8, 2020

Vanessa spent the weekend resting at home with Jenny Wang spoiling her. As Jenny was massaging her neck, Vanessa's phone rang. She recognized the incoming number but decided to play dumb.

'Hi, this is Julie. '

'Julie Ma? This is Diane Ramsay.'

'Diane Ramsay? I'm sorry, I don't recognize your name. What can I do for you? Please be quick, I'm busy.'

'You do recognize my name, don't you? Remember Julie? You contacted me by email some months ago with an offer to *arrange matters*, as you put it, for me and Lania Sharkey. We agreed on a deal, remember? A real simple deal. All I had to do was confirm Sharkey's death with a simple *yes*, when you called. Which I did, at the hospital on that fateful Friday the thirteenth of November when Luke Sharkey died with Covid. Remember now, Ms. Ma? The same Ms. Julie Ma who gave Tom Wood those poisoned capsules that Sharkey inhaled for his asthma condition before he died? I'm sure the police will be fascinated by this interesting set of coincidences.'

'I don't know what you're talking about Miss Ramsay.'

'Listen here Ma. I know what you did, and I know what you're up to now. You will not get away with this. What you don't know is that I have a sample of Sharkey's urine. Lania got it for me, before he died. Urine contains traces of whatever was in his blood that you used to poison him. So don't send that video to the police, otherwise I will tell them what you did. Tom Wood just told me all about your devious scheme to implicate him and me for the murder of Luke Sharkey.'

'Miss Ramsay, I have no idea what you are talking about and I'm going to hang up the phone now and block your number.'

'That urine sample proves that Sharkey did *not* die of natural causes. This means the legal contract that your uncle has with Sharkey will no longer be valid, so he won't get control of Sharkey's property empire. Your uncle's plan will collapse, and he will not be a happy man. All those years of planning will come to nothing, Ms. Ma.'

'I don't know who you are Miss Ramsay, nor what you're talking about. I am now going to hang up.'

'I'm prepared to negotiate. The urine sample is in a safe place. You can have it, for a price. My opening bid is two million pounds sterling. What's your offer?'

Vanessa pressed the red button on her i-phone and signaled to Jenny to continue massaging her neck.

'Stupid woman. She's out of her league.'

Vanessa then called a number already logged into her phone contacts. It was Joe Sharkey, Luke's uncle.

Fifty-Seven

Monday afternoon, December 8, 2020

Sanjay Singh and Steve Whittley knocked on Tom Wood's apartment door in Walker Square. They were both masked due to the continuing Covid restrictions.

'Police. I'm DI Whittley and this is Sergeant Singh. Can we come in?'

Tom opened the door looking as though he'd just got out of bed, even though it was two o'clock in the afternoon. He had a scar around his lips, where some hairs had been torn out. Had he been burnt, Steve thought?

Steve didn't show his warrant card because he no longer had it. DCI McCartney had taken it on the night he'd been suspended and had stored it in his safe in his office.

Luckily Tom let them in without asking for any proof of identity.

'Drink, gentlemen?' Tom poured himself a large whisky, without waiting for an answer to his own question. He invited Steve and Sanjay to be seated on a grey sofa that had seen better days.

'What can I do for you? How can I be of help?'

Steve had explained to Sanjay beforehand that he would do all the talking. Better not risk any slip-ups, and Steve was used to the sort of aggressive questioning he'd planned for this session.

'Mr. Wood, we have strong evidence to believe you were involved in the murder of Mr. Luke Sharkey.'

'Murder? What murder? My friend Luke died with Covid. Haven't you read the papers?'

'That's what the public thinks. We know otherwise.'

Of course, neither Steve nor Sanjay had any proof that Luke had been murdered. They were just using common police questioning techniques of lying to pry out the truth from their suspect. In this case they wanted to question Tom about the video Jane had extracted from his phone. They suspected that the asthma capsules had been tampered with, but they had no proof.

The goal of their questioning was to examine Tom's reaction to all potential accusations they threw at him, including spiking the capsules.

With what poison? They didn't know and would be hard-pressed to prove anything.

Sharkey's body had been cremated very soon after he'd died. And because the medics had thought he'd died with Covid, there had been no autopsy. Whatever. This afternoon they intended to shake Tom up a bit to see what came out. They were hoping that Tom would confess to Sharkey's murder, or at least let something slip.

Wood seemed genuinely surprised when Steve explained that Sharkey had not died with Covid.

'How did he die then?'

'Well, not from Covid that's for sure,' Steve replied.

'The police do know that Sharkey had asthma, don't they?' Tom said. 'People with asthma have a much higher chance of dying from Covid.'

'Is that right, Mr. Wood?'

'I must have read it somewhere, I guess. Wikipedia, I think.'

Steve continued his probing. 'So how do you know Mr. Sharkey had asthma?'

'Most people knew, I think. He often had his emergency inhaler with him. We chatted a few times about this. My brother also suffers from asthma, and I sometimes get his meds from the pharmacy. Like Luke, he uses both corticosteroids and Indacaterol. They both come in capsule form and the medicine is delivered through inhalers.'

Steve now went for the jugular. 'Mr. Wood, we have strong reason to believe that you and Miss Diane Ramsay spiked Mr. Luke Sharkey's asthma capsules intending to kill him. Is that the case?'

Tom's face went white. 'What do you mean, spike? Yes, I gave Diane some capsules, but I didn't know that they were spiked. With what?'

Steve kept pushing. 'Who gave you the capsules in the first place?'

'I'm not going to answer that. And by the way, I never asked you to show me your warrant cards. So go on, I want to see them. How do I know your real coppers? I invited you into my house to help you, not to be accused of some crime I didn't commit.'

At this point Sanjay interjected. 'Mr. Wood, you've been very helpful. We're very sorry if we upset you. We didn't mean to. Sometimes we are forced to be cruel to be kind. Just part of the job we do is to protect and serve the great British public. You know that. We'll be on our way now. If you have any additional information, please contact our IT expert on this number. She is collating all the data around this nasty business. Have a good day Mr. Wood.'

After handing Tom Jane Wilson's call card, Sanjay and Steve saw themselves out.

Fifty-Eight

Tuesday afternoon, December 9, 2020

The next afternoon Steve paid a visit to Diane Ramsay. Her apartment was in a different block to Tom Wood's in Walker Square.

Earlier that day Jane Wilson had done something she hoped she'd never regret. She'd entered the half-deserted Merseyside Police HQ and taken Steve's warrant card from the safe in DCI McCartney's office. Only DCI McCartney knew the code to the safe. He'd noted down the number on a simple Word document with all his passwords on his PC hard drive, which was automatically copied every day to the central server. Could he have made it any easier for an IT whizz like Jane?

To get into the building Steve needed either the code or a fob to swipe the magnetic reader, which opened the door automatically. He had neither. He didn't want to use the intercom to call Diane as he was counting on an element of surprise and wanted to gauge her visual expressions when they met. Luckily, as he arrived at the door, a resident was leaving, and he was able to slip in behind her before the door closed.

He decided to walk up the three floors to Diane's apartment. When he got there, the door was slightly ajar. Is she in? Should I announce myself? What the hell, let's take a chance, thought Steve. Sanjay had told him she kept Sharkey's urine sample somewhere in her flat, probably in the fridge, or maybe the bathroom.

He took the chance and entered the apartment. Diane was not there. For a full five minutes Steve scoured the place but did not find any urine sample. He even sniffed what appeared to be some apple juice in the fridge, only to find that it was precisely that, apple juice!

As he was walking out, Diane arrived with a basket full of laundry.

'Who the hell are you and what are you doing in my apartment? Get out, immediately, or else I'll call the police!"

'Sorry to frighten you, Miss Ramsay. I am the police. DI Whittley from Merseyside Police.'

Steve showed Diane his warrant card.

'Why are you here and do you have a search warrant? You can't just barge into my apartment like that. It's illegal.'

Steve replied that he'd seen the door ajar and had entered because he was worried Diane may be injured, explaining that there could be people who wanted to hurt her, following Luke Sharkey's death. He told Diane about the video he'd seen in which Tom Wood had given her some asthma-treatment capsules, and asked her if she remembered this?

Diane sat down at the kitchen table with her head in her hands for a few silent minutes.

Steve gave her a glass of water and asked her if she needed anything else.

'No thanks. What I need is a break from all this mess. Lania's gone and you're treating me like a prime suspect for a crime I know nothing about.'

'What do you mean?' replied Steve.

'All I know is that Tom Wood gave me asthma capsules. His brother suffers from asthma, just like Luke Sharkey. Lania, my friend, is married to Luke. Tom had told Lania, who works at his club, about this new brand, which is much more effective. They've been recently authorized by the FDA for use in the USA. Tom said he'd found some online and wanted to give them to Lania for Luke. I just happened to be in the club when Tom was around and he gave the sample to me.'

'Sounds quite complicated. Did you pass the sample on to Lania?'

'I'm sorry officer, but I can't say any more. Something frightening happened to me on Saturday afternoon. I came home and found out that someone had broken into my apartment. That's why the door was open. They broke the lock. I haven't had time to fix it and the property management company here is useless.'

'What did the police say when you reported the break-in?'

'I haven't reported it yet.'

'Why not?'

'Not worth it. Your lot never find the burglars in any case.'

'Did anything go missing?'

'Yes. Well, no, nothing really.'

'Is that a yes, or a no?'

'No. Nothing went missing.'

Steve decided to increase the pressure.

'Nothing went missing, eh? Not even a container of urine? A sample of Luke Sharkey's urine that your lover Lania, Luke's wife, took from him before he died, Miss Ramsay?'

'I don't know what you are talking about.'

'Oh, but I think you do. We have a witness who heard you on the night of Sharkey's death asking Lania if she'd got the urine sample.'

'Who's your witness?'

'You think I'm going to tell you that Miss Ramsay? Aiding and abetting a murder carries a stiff sentence. At least three years. You can make it much easier for yourself if you go down to the police station straight away and make your statement to PC Jane Wilson. She's waiting for you there. The judge will certainly be more lenient with your sentence if you do as we say.'

'Look, it's pretty simple. I have no urine sample of Luke Sharkey. Why would I? What would I have to gain by that?'

'Maybe the urine sample contains proof that Mr. Sharkey was murdered and did not die with Covid. Maybe inside the capsules that you gave Lania contained other substances. Poisonous substances that killed Luke Sharkey?'

'And why would I want him dead?'

'That's the easy part, Miss Ramsay. You had a strong motive. You're having a relationship with his wife, Lania. My guess is that Luke took out a good life insurance policy for her. And you both stand to gain from that now, don't you? We all know that Sharkey was a difficult man. He was a total jerk if you ask me. I know that from firsthand experience. It's because of him that my damned boss suspended me.'

It took Steve just a split second to realize what he'd just said. But it was too late. Diane had heard him, loud and clear.

'Suspended? You're suspended? You have a nerve. Walking into my apartment, accusing me of murder. Get out! Get out at once! I will report you immediately to the police. You're going to be in very big trouble mister suspended policeman, very soon. Now get out!'

Steve had no choice. Stupid. How could he be so dumb? He'd let his anger and emotion get to him. Big mistake.

Steve left the building quickly, walked down Hanover Street and crossed the road towards the Albert Dock. Where was Sanjay? He'd said he'd gone for a walk along the river. North, or South direction?

Just as Steve was about to get out his mobile, he saw Sanjay walking towards him.

'What's up, no balls? Looks like you've seen a ghost. Is Luke Sharkey spooking you? I've seen his ghost a few times as well since he died.'

'I've effed up big time Sanj. Big time.'

'Again?'

'No joking please, it's not funny, mate. When I was interviewing Diane Ramsay, I stupidly let it slip that I'm suspended from the force. No surprise, she kicked me out of her apartment there and then and told me she'd be notifying the police.'

'She won't, no balls. No way. I tell you she won't. She's bluffing. She's got too much to hide. Guess you didn't find the urine sample, eh?'

'No. But someone had broken into her apartment last Saturday. She didn't report it to the police.'

'I told you. She's got too much to hide. I wonder if that someone who broke into her apartment stole the urine sample. Get my drift Steve?'

'Yep, it adds up nicely Sanj. But who?'

Fifty-Nine

Wednesday morning, December 10, 2020, London

Andy Backland and Joe Sharkey got off the train in Euston station, London, just before midday. They'd travelled first class from Liverpool Lime Street. Money was no object anymore. They knew they were about to come into some big money.

They took a taxi to Silk Street, to the offices of the UK's leading company law solicitors, Berkeley Payne, where Vanessa Chan had asked to meet up.

The law firm's porter showed them into a conference room that looked like it hadn't changed in over one hundred years, the walls lined with oak and mahogany panelling and the shelves stacked with old books. It certainly set the scene well.

Vanessa Chan entered the room, followed by her uncle, Mr. Benny Zhang and the solicitor handling the case for Berkeley Payne, Mr. Jeffrey Salt.

Seated around the beautifully crafted teak table each person gave a short personal introduction and Jeffrey Salt officially opened the proceedings, referring to the meeting agenda that Vanessa had given him in advance.

At this point Mr. Zhang interrupted Salt. 'Mr. Salt. Thank you very much for all the preparation that you've made. Before we move on to the finer details of the contract, could you please give us a minute?'

'No problem, Mr. Zhang. Give me a sign when you need me back.'

Salt left the room, leaving the two parties face-to-face across the table.

Zhang kicked off the discussions. 'It is, of course, a great pleasure to meet you both in person. I believe that we can work out a very fair deal between us, but I think that your 50/50 proposition is unreasonable and unworkable. It's always better to have a majority partner to move the business forward and to take the hard decisions. With respect, gentlemen, I have much more experience in property than both of you, as I'm sure you'll appreciate. Sixty-forty would work much better.'

Replying to this, Joe Sharkey said 'Mr. Zhang. No problem whatsoever with sixty-forty, as long as we're the sixty and you're the forty. You must understand that we have all the winning cards now. With the urine sample stocked away in very safekeeping, we can prove without any shadow of a doubt that my dearest nephew, Luke Sharkey, did not die of natural causes. This completely nullifies your legal contract with him whereby you'd inherit all his properties if he dies before you, but only of *natural causes.*'

'Vanessa, do you have any thoughts on this?' Zhang knew deep down that fifty-fifty would be a good deal and was prepared to sign, but he wanted to make his new partners sweat a little more.

'Uncle Benny. I've been working on this deal for many years now. And I truly see a great future in property development in the great city of Liverpool. What counts less than the shareholder split is our joint strategy, moving forward. I believe that I am well-placed to design this future strategy and would like to propose myself as the Chief Executive Officer of this company.'

Joe Sharkey nodded in full agreement. 'This only makes sense, of course, if I'm the Chairman. You can count on me to be hands-off. I have plenty of other business to take care of as a member of Liverpool City Council. The city is expanding and, as a born and bred Liverpudlian, I need to play my part.'

'Ok, then,' Zhang said, 'as long as my niece becomes the CEO, I'll accept your proposed fifty-fifty share split. We can work out the Articles of Association later.'

'Seems like we've got a deal then. Shall I ask Mr. Salt to return?' Andy Backland got up and left to fetch Jeffrey Salt back into the room.

'Thank you, gentlemen. All's well that ends well,' concluded Vanessa, the newly nominated CEO, lapping up every joyful second.

At last, payback time. She was the CEO of a major player in property development in the northwest of England, and this was just the beginning of her conquest.

'With your permission, I'll start working on the press release. We'll begin with my favourite rag, the *Liverpool Post*. A young English literature graduate from the University of Oxford, Sarah Baxter, has just started her journalism career there. I'll reach out to her asap. Would be good to have her on our side from the get-go.'

Sixty

Saturday morning, December 13, 2020, Sanjay's apartment, Liverpool City Centre

Steve had hurried round to Sanjay's apartment after their early morning telephone discussion, Sanjay was distressed and needed comfort.

Steve sat himself down on the sofa and sipped the espresso Sanjay had served him.

'No, I haven't read the article yet Sanjay,' Steve said.

'Can you believe it? My managing editor gave this Sarah Baxter rookie the scoop instead of me. The girl's not even out of diapers. What does she even know about our city, she grew up in Guildford, for God's sake, and went to some posh school? Makes me want to puke, Steve. After all those years toiling away, delivering more scoops than any other *Post* journalist ever, this is how I'm treated.'

'Disgusting, I agree mate. You need to take the editor aside and have a strong word. Tell him about your network and your inside contacts, like me. It'll take years for this Baxter woman to build that up.'

'I'll give her six months, max. In her article she talks about a certain Vanessa Chan. Never come across that name before. Have you?'

'Sure. Vanessa Chan. Didn't I brief you about her, Sanj? Apologies. Give me a minute to read the article and I'll tell you all I know about Vanessa Chan.' Steve picked up the *Post* and read at the front-page headline out loud.

Just reward for Uncle Joe as Chinese capital re-floats Sharkey Group
Moving to the inside pages, he began to read the rest.

Hi there all! I'm your new business columnist, Sarah Baxter, and I'm bringing you some important breaking news for our great city.

Following an exclusive interview in London with the new owners, I can reveal that the Sharkey Group, built from scratch by our own born-and-bred Liverpool man, the late Luke Sharkey, will remain in the hands of our city's brightest and best.

Effective today, Mr. Joe Sharkey, the late founder's uncle, has been named Chairman of the Sharkey Group. He has appointed Ms. Vanessa Chan, a law graduate from the University of Liverpool, as the Group's new Chief Executive

Officer. With her extensive international network, Chan will ensure a stronger flow of capital into the Group and into our city, from Chinese investors specifically. This will help boost Liverpool's reputation as the Shanghai of Great Britain, significantly enhancing our city's prospects as we move towards mid-century 2021, the so-called Asian Century.

Reinforcing the local roots of the company, Liverpool Mayor Don Ferguson, the City Council's Head of Regeneration, Mickey Cavandish, along with local solicitor Andy Backland have all been appointed to the Sharkey Group's Board of Directors.

Steve didn't need to read the rest of the article. The picture had suddenly become very clear, and he felt both relieved and excited. The culprits had come forth. Time now to bang them up.

But there was just one problem: evidence!

Sanjay was still fuming. 'Still don't believe it Steve. How can they give that story to Sarah Baxter, from Guildford? It's just outrageous. She didn't even study journalism at university.'

Steve gave a long shushing sound with his index finger and started to slowly explain the situation to a very angry Sanjay.

'I understand that you're upset Sanj. Let's take a step back from our personal feelings. Objectively speaking, this is the best piece of news that we've had in our investigation so far. Why? Because we've found the link that we were missing all along. The link between Vanessa Chan and Joe Sharkey.'

'Enlighten me, no balls.'

'Jane Wilson did some research on that student, Julia Ma. She's the woman who was saved from drowning by my gallant brother the other week in Crosby. Turns out her real name is Vanessa Chan, the niece of Benny Zhang, a very big property tycoon from Beijing, China.'

'So what?'

'I'm piecing the puzzle together as we speak. She's now been appointed CEO of the Sharkey Group 2.0 by Joe Sharkey and Benny Zhang. Why? It's not just about bringing in more Chinese capital into the company, is it?'

'You think it's related to Sharkey's murder Steve?'

'I do. Just follow my logic for a minute. You told me about the urine sample discussion at the hospital when Sharkey was dying, remember?

174

You said that Diane Ramsay kept it in her flat, and then we speculated that someone broke in and stole it from her apartment.'

'That's right, and I still think it's significant.'

'It's more than significant Sanj. It's the most important connection that we have. Remember, it was Diane who was keeping the sample in her fridge. Why? To blackmail someone, we figured.'

'*I* figured, you mean.' Sanjay was beginning to understand the bigger picture that Steve was painting.

'And who do you think Diane Ramsay wanted to blackmail, Sanjay?'

'Vanessa Chan? I guess that's where your logic is taking you. But I don't yet know why?' Sanjay answered.

'Because Vanessa Chan wanted Sharkey dead. Period.'

'And why would she want him dead? Do we have any evidence of that?'

'No. It's just a supposition for the moment. But my copper's nose tells me it's true.'

'We're going to need more than that, Steve.'

'I know. We need to speak to Lania Sharkey. Maybe Joe Sharkey was in cahoots with her, who knows?'

Suddenly Steve's phone started vibrating. It was Jane Wilson. He pressed the green button and put her on the loudspeaker.

'Hi there, boss. About Lania. Not good news I'm afraid. She's left the country. She took the life insurance money and fled back to Venezuela, a country which does not have an extradition treaty with the UK.'

'That's all we need Jane. Bloody hell!' Steve yelled down the phone.

'Sorry, boss.

'No Jane, it's me who's sorry. Not your fault is it?' Steve said, realizing that he'd screamed at her very unreasonably down the phone.

'Looks like she's taken her secrets with her,' Sanjay added, with a disappointed look on his face. 'Anything else, Jane?'

'Yes boss. Diane Ramsay. She's not who she seems to be either. She has a history of befriending vulnerable wives of rich men. Three years ago, she was taken to court by a London stockbroker for harassing his much younger wife, but the judge acquitted her. And there have been several other dubious cases, but nothing serious enough to warrant her arrest and question her.'

'So that's two potential witnesses out of the window. What else? Make my day!'

'That's it for now Steve. I'll keep searching. I never give up boss.'

Steve pressed the red button on his phone.

'Shit, shit, shit!'

'And shit,' Sanjay added.

'You know something Sanj, sometimes I think that there is no justice in this world. We're being played. By Vanessa Chan. By Diane Ramsay. By Tom Wood. And the true villain of the sage, the sly and slippery uncle, councilman Joe Sharkey.'

'What's your take on him Steve, the uncle?'

'I'm certain he's schemed his way into a fortune he could never have dreamt of while his nephew was alive.'

'You could well be right, mate.'

'Problem is, Sanj, I'll never be reinstated until we prove Sharkey's murder and found out who did it.'

Sanjay was feeling sorry for Steve. Yes, that upstart Sarah Baxter had just stolen his crime scene, but at least he still had his job, and this was just a temporary setback, for sure. Steve was still suspended and it looked like it would stay that way.

'You know what I think Steve. More often than not these days, crime pays. Especially fraud.'

'That's a fact. A sad fact,' Steve replied.

The two of them sat there for a while in silence.

Then Sanjay said, philosophically, 'Luke Sharkey may no longer be with us Steve, but his ghost will haunt this city for years to come.'

'Dead right. He's been haunting me since McCartney messed up Sharkey's apartment search warrant.'

'Time to change the scenery, no balls. We never did get round to watching the greatest cricket match of all time, did we? That blast from the past. The Botham test, 1981, when we were still in short pants and I was knocking you for six. I've still got the DVD. You gave it to me as a birthday present, remember? I'll get the beers from the fridge. Life's a short innings and then you die.'

PART FOUR
SPRING 2021

Sixty-One

Liverpool, Spring, 2021

Five months had passed since Jane, Sanjay and Steve had come to the sad conclusion that they'd probably never find enough evidence to implicate anyone in the murder of Luke Sharkey.

Jane and Sanjay had returned to their offices; Steve's office was both at home *and* at the Albert Dock as a tourist guide.

Since the successful national vaccination programme and the easing of Covid restrictions, the Albert Dock had become busy again with tourists. With a difference this time: almost all visitors were domestic. Foreigners were still prohibited from entering the country. The Brexiteers must be very happy, thought Steve.

The country was wallowing in a new-found, but short-lived pride in their health authorities, which had organised the double Covid vaccination of over half the population at rapid speed. Much quicker than those Johnny Foreigners in Europe. Brexit justified, they cried.

Along with around sixty percent of fellow residents of Liverpool, Steve had voted to remain *inside* the European Union in that crazy referendum. That was now ancient history and he'd reluctantly accepted the result, though he maintained it was a pyrrhic victory for the Leave camp.

With his top-mop of grey hair growing longer each day, Steve was back down at the Albert Dock with the day's tourist catch. Today it was a group of retired teachers from the Southampton area, a port city five hours away by bus on the south coast of England.

Steve was enjoying this work and making a lot of money for his chosen charity, Shelter.

He was in the middle of some history, explaining that both port cities had been massively bombed in the Second World War, when his phone rang. It was Jane Wilson. She'd not been in contact since the beginning of the year. They'd agreed she'd only call if she had vitally important new evidence in the Sharkey case.

'Give me ten minutes Jane and I'll call you back,' replied Steve excitedly, before escorting the group to the corner of the Albert Dock and giving them fifteen minutes to explore on their own. He asked them to meet back up at the *Beatles Story*.

'What's up Jane? We agreed that you'd only contact me if you'd found important new evidence, right?'

'That's right boss, and I have, boss. We need to meet. Come round to our house this afternoon. No worries, Steve, we're both vaxed and waxed,' Jane joked.

Steve grabbed a takeaway coffee and immediately sent a text message asking Sanjay to join the meeting at Jane's at two pm.

After the *Beatles* tour, Steve said goodbye to his guests, who'd been very generous with their offerings to Shelter. Walking towards his car there was a tune that he couldn't get out of his head, *The Long and Winding Road*. Another great *Beatles* song. The title seemed very appropriate for what Steve was going through at present. He crossed his fingers and hoped that Jane's new evidence would lead him to the door, finally.

Sixty-Two

Wednesday early afternoon, April 14, 2021, Jane and Crys' House, Sefton, Liverpool

Sanjay had already arrived when Steve rang the front doorbell. Jane shouted instructions to let himself in and to come over to the backroom, her home office.

Steve pulled up a chair to the right of Jane seated at her computer, with Sanjay on her left. They both looked avidly at the screen while Jane explained what was to follow.

'Gentlemen,' began Jane, 'I'm about to pull up a QR code on the screen. You know what that is. You've both been vaxed, and the NHS issued you a QR code as proof of your vaccination status. A QR code can serve many purposes. For our purposes today the QR code is an electronic key giving access to some other piece of digital information which sends an instruction to something, or someone else.'

'Got it,' Steve said confidently, clearly lying through his teeth.

'The QR code you now see on screen' Jane continued, 'is quite a discovery, gentlemen.'

'Where did you find it?' asked Steve.

'Remember that fateful raid on Sharkey's house last year? The one that eventually led to your wrongful suspension. The one where our great leader McCartney messed up like never before.'

'How could I forget Jane?'

'Well, as is my wont, I did a lot of snooping around Sharkey's apartment that night after you'd left and I took a load of photos. In Sharkey's bedside table drawer, I found this QR code stuck to a piece of plastic. It looked harmless enough, and up until now I'd assumed it must have been some sort of discount supermarket card, so I did no further research.'

'And then?' interjected Sanjay.

'And then I had eureka moment. When I received my NHS Covid QR code after my second vaccination it dawned on me that maybe the QR code I found Sharkey's was more than a discount voucher.'

'And?' Steve panted, like a dog waiting for a treat.

'And it turns out that this QR code holds the key to the secret bank account of Luke Sharkey, at Coopers Bank on Hanover Street. This QR code opens the box in the bank vault which Sharkey used to store his most secret documents.'

'We must get down to Coopers Bank immediately.'

'No need, boss. I've already been. The manager was very accommodating. She simply scanned the code, took me down to the vaults, where she scanned the code again, and a small safe in the corner automatically opened. She then left me to it.'

'What did you find?'

'A USB stick.'

'That's it,' Steve said in disbelief, 'just one measly little Usb stick?'

'I don't know what's on it yet, boss. I thought I'd better wait for you to inspect it.'

'OK, good decision Jane. Let's look, now, this minute, without delay.'

The three of them spent the next six hours poring over file after file, watching the videos, and listening to all of the audio files on the twenty Giga USB stick.

At seven pm, Steve got up from his chair and stretched his whole torso, letting out a massive, bear-like groan. It was a sigh of enormous satisfaction and relief.

'GOTCHA!' he yelled.

Sixty-Three

Saturday evening, April 17, 2021, Philharmonic Dining Rooms, Hope Street, Liverpool

Mayor Don Ferguson and Joe Sharkey along with Andy Backland and Mickey Cavandish, had invited all their friends and colleagues to a lavish Saturday evening celebration at the Philharmonic Dining Rooms on Hope Street. They'd rented the whole historic building for the evening and had spared no expense for the official launch of the Sharkey Group 2.0, as the company was now called. They'd even succeeded in luring the presence of BBC Northwest, a local TV station with a news audience of several million across the region.

Once all the city's makers and shakers had arrived, including the managers of both Everton and Liverpool football clubs, Joe Sharkey took the microphone.

'Ladies and gentlemen, a warm welcome to you all at this, the official launch of the Sharkey Group 2.0. Firstly, our Liverpool-educated CEO, Vanessa Chan, sends her sincere apologies for not being here with us today. As we speak, she is in our nation's capital already at work on creating the international arm of our Group, with a view to a London Stock Exchange listing within the next five years.

Yes, ladies and gentlemen, we are ambitious. Ambitious for our city. Ambitious for our investors. And, most of all, we are ambitious for you, our partners, and our staff.

My nephew, the late and great Luke Sharkey, created this company from nothing and built it up to where it is now. I feel truly honoured that he chose to leave the company in my hands should he ever pass away before me, which should never have happened. Before I continue, let's have a moment of silence in his honour.'

The background buzz immediately dissipated, and the room fell silent. The only perceptible noise was at the sound desk where two people were whispering to the engineer.

After thirty seconds, Joe Sharkey resumed.

'In the natural order of things, it would be Luke at my place today heralding this new chapter in the company's development. But tragedy hit, and his frail chest, already suffering chronic asthma, succumbed to that most horrible of viruses, Covid.

I know that he's looking down on us from up there wishing us well and shouting Come On You Blues! No offence to the reds among us this evening of course, Jurgen. Before I hand over to our Mayor, please join me in a toast. To Luke. Luke Sharkey. The best player Everton never had and to his naturally generous, optimistic attitude towards love and life. To Luke!'

While the *hoi polloi* were busy toasting, DCI McCartney and PC Jane Wilson gave the thumbs up to the sound engineer. Sanjay and Steve watched from the back of the ornate Victorian bar.

Mayor Ferguson was on next. He took the stage and tested his microphone, but it wasn't working. He made a couple of gestures to the sound engineer, who ignored him.

At that moment, the speaker volume was turned up and a voice which was certainly not the Mayor's began to be piped through the system.

People started chatting among themselves. Who is it? I recognise that voice. How could it be? Isn't he dead?

Suddenly, the room became eerily quiet as people began to recognise the voice coming through the speakers. There was no mistaking. It was Luke Sharkey, no doubt about it.

I'm living my life to the full now. My company is successful and will grow to be Britain's biggest property development corporation ever.

I have everyone I need in my pocket. The Mayor, the City Regeneration Head, and many of the city councillors. Thanks to them selling me the freeholds for peanuts, I'm now a rich man. And they are rich too.

I'm recording these files as a safeguard in case anybody tries to screw me. Apart from my mother, I don't trust anyone, not even my uncle Joe.

In a file on this USB stick you will find all the necessary paperwork proving that the Mayor, Uncle Joe, Mickey Cavandish and others all have secret bank accounts in Panama set up by yours truly. Each month they receive payments for their services directly to their personal offshore accounts. No traceability. No taxes. No worries for them. Except, that is, if they betray me, which is why I record this log every day in my bedroom.

As the audio file was playing through the speakers, a red-faced Mayor Ferguson stormed over to the sound engineer and started to physically threaten him. DCI McCartney, of course, had anticipated this and a couple of his beefier PCs quickly had the old Mayor under control. Mickey Cavandish and Andy Backland had remained in place at the front, with their wives staring at them in disbelief. Uncle Joe Sharkey had retreated to the bar and was stooped with his head in his hands. Sanjay, Steve, and Jane had regrouped next to the sound system and could not conceal their joy.

The recording continued.

Today, Andy Backland and I met with Vanessa Chan and her uncle, Mr. Benny Zhang. We made a total no-brainer of a deal. I couldn't believe it. Benny is seventy years old, if he's a day, probably more. He's just signed a contract in which he's literally giving me millions of pounds to invest in my properties, as I wish. The only proviso is that if I die of natural causes before him, he will inherit my company. Yes, you heard that right, natural causes! Fat chance of that. I'm not even forty yet. And old fella Zhang is a chain-smoker. Naturally, I signed the deal. He'll die before me and I'll have pocketed his cash, for free.

Andy Backland put down his champagne glass and moved surreptitiously towards the exit, only to be apprehended by another of McCartney's heavier-set PCs. The recording continued.

And I'm defo not handing my company over to Uncle Joe, since he abused me as a kid, bastard. Messed me up for a long time, he did. I only use him for his connections at the council, but after that I'd rather see him dead, which I will, when we eventually get to payback time.

A suppressed *ooh* spread through the room. It was as if Uncle Joe, stooped even further at the bar, was somehow expecting this revelation. He made no attempt to leave, or to resist the approaching police constable.

The recording continued.

Mayor Ferguson. If you're listening, let me thank you once again. I know we didn't do things by the book, but what the hell, we're building the new Liverpool. All those local folk we employ. The end justifies the means, that's what I say. As for all those foreign investors, they've got plenty of money. They'll survive. And Mayor, I'd also like to thank your son for his help in transferring the money to Panama. He was the best mule you could ever want for and great company on those flights out there not to mention in the clubs we visited.

At this point Mayor Ferguson shouted 'You leave my son out of this. He's innocent. Done nothing wrong. And neither have I. I've just done the best for the city I love. My city, my people. And get your hands off me..' at which point two police officers escorted the protesting Mayor to the awaiting van, outside the Rooms.

DCI McCartney decided that this was enough drama for one evening and asked the sound engineer to transfer the channel to the microphone in his hand.

'Ladies and gentlemen, this is Detective Chief Inspector McCartney of Merseyside Police. We are sorry to have interrupted your evening, but I'm sure you'll appreciate why. I'm asking you all to now leave the premises in a calm and orderly fashion. Given what you've witnessed this evening, I would also invite you to come by our HQ or call us over the next few days with any additional information you may have related to this case. Your contact person is Jane Wilson, standing to my right. Have a safe trip home, ladies and gentlemen. Thank you for your attention.'

Sixty-Four

Monday morning, April 19, 2021, Merseyside Police HQ, Liverpool

DCI McCartney convened all the Operation Croft team, as well as Steve Whittley and Sanjay Singh for a debriefing that Monday morning.

The lovely Spring weather matched the success of the previous Saturday's operation at the Philharmonic Rooms. Blue sky and no rain. OK, there was a chilly breeze coming off the river, but it was good, clear, clean air, justifying Liverpool's reputation as the city with the best quality air in England.

It had been Jane Wilson's idea to gatecrash the Sharkey Group 2.0's launch party and to publicly humiliate the new management team. DCI McCartney had contacted his local television and print media contacts, giving them enough preliminary bait as to ensure their presence for this fantastic scoop.

It had certainly been effective. BBC Northwest had pushed the story onto London, and it had even been broadcast on BBC World News. Many of Sharkey's original investors in Malaysia, the Middle East, Singapore, and Hong Kong had watched the news item and had already sent congratulatory emails to DCI McCartney. Many of them expressed relief and a renewed faith in the British justice system, which McCartney relayed on to the team in his opening remarks.

Having thanked the team and explained the next steps for the prosecution of the culprits, McCartney pressed a button on his i-phone, which was connected to a UE Boom speaker. He was beginning to get a taste for the dramatic!

'And now, dear colleagues, *la pièce maîtresse*. On the same USB stick that our friend Luke Sharkey stored secretly in the bank vault was another audio file, one we didn't play to the public last Saturday evening. Seems like Lania, Sharkey's wife, was somewhat smarter than we thought. Not just a pretty face, you could say.'

There was an embarrassed mumbling as he said the bit about the pretty face. McCartney had not yet fully digested the learnings of his unconscious bias course.

He continued.

'After her husband's death, Lania Sharkey went to the bank and added her interpretation of events. Lania had a bonafide copy of the QR code, which was all she needed to access the bank vault. She recorded her own audio file on the USB stick, then put it back into the bank vault. Ladies and gentlemen, I give you Lania. Lania Sharkey. Or is it back to Lania *Reyes* now?'

A woman's voice with a soft Latin American, Spanish-language accent started to pipe through the speakers.

Hello DCI McCartney, hello Steve, Sanjay and Jane. This is Lania. I guess my accent gives me away, ha! When you listen to this recording, I will be back in Venezuela on an island called Margherita in our beautiful Caribbean Sea. Bet you can't guess what I'll be drinking!

There is no extradition treaty between Venezuela and the UK. So don't come after me. Now I'm rich, I don't need to ever leave my home country again. Ownership of the Bearer Shares I took from the Coopers Bank vault safe, before you visited, mean I'm now the sole owner of the millions that Sharkey hid in Panama.

No, he never mentioned to me he had a secret box in the vaults at Coopers Bank. No surprise there. Luckily for me, a kind and gentle homeless man I befriended in the city told me he often saw Luke at the bank's branch on Hanover Street. The one where they have the vaults. Pretty-faced Lania put two and two together, didn't she?

I'm now looking after Kevin Day, financially speaking that is. Poor man, his dog died recently, and he's devastated. I've bought him a little terraced house in Wavertree and I video chat with him every month. I'm also financing 24/7 care for the man. He deserves it after everything he's gone through. You'll be pleased to know he's off the booze and cleaning up his act.

I guess I could have pushed for more money from Luke's property empire. When Vanessa Chan approached me with her plan to kill Luke and pass it off for Covid, she offered me a substantial stake in the Sharkey Group. I was tempted. She told me about the contract her uncle had with Luke and that she'd make me a co-owner. Alas for me this meant remaining in Liverpool, which I didn't want to do. I figured that there was enough in Luke's secret bank accounts in Panama to support me, having found those Bearer Shares. Oh, and yes, I also got a nice little life insurance payout. It'll help pay my beach house utility bills. Sorry Diane! You can now move on to your next victim. Never underestimate a pretty face, my sweet.

Vanessa explained to me how she intended to murder my dear husband. Pretty simple really. Replace the powder in Luke's asthma treatment capsules with the right dose of moleculized Ricin, and hey presto, he's gone. And it worked like a dream. Ricin is a derivative of linseed. You police people probably know that secret services have been using it for years, the most famous being the assassination in the late nineteen seventies of a Bulgarian dissident, Georgi Ivanov Markov. He was killed on a street in the capital with a micro-engineered Ricin pellet stabbed into him on the end of an umbrella. That was much more James Bond than our ugly solution, capsules in an inhaler. But who cares? It's the result that counts.

Vanessa blackmailed Tom Wood, who gave the capsules to Diane and then on to me. Diane didn't think I knew about any of this. Ha! When she asked me to get a urine sample from Luke before he died, I'd already figured out her devious plan. She needed something to prove that Ricin killed Luke, and not Covid. Tom had told Diane about Vanessa's plan. They all thought I was a fool and would never discover anything.

Never underestimate a pretty Venezuelan woman!

Initially, Tom and Diane tried to have Vanessa drowned, roped to those stupid statues in that murky river Mersey. Guess they didn't reckon on Jenny Wang and the hero of the day, Nick Whittley, your brother, Steve! What a hero. Give him a medal.

Uncle Joe? You'll have to ask him how he knew about all this. I don't know how close he was to Vanessa Chan. Then again, why did he insist on rapidly cremating my darling Luke, when burial is the family tradition? Probably to stop an autopsy taking place to find the Ricin. That's my guess.

Diane thought she was smart in keeping that urine sample in the fridge. Ha! When I told Uncle Joe about this, anonymously of course, all her blackmail plans were thwarted. No less than she deserved, trying to hide her past from me as she did.

Uncle Joe will be pleased to see that I wear great nanna's wedding ring every day. Mother Mary told me the secret of the moonstone set into the ring; it brings the wearer fertility and riches. Well, Luke, I've got the money now, guess I'll have to start working on the children. Sorry you won't be the father babe, but that's life. You live by the sword; you die by it.

DCI McCartney pressed the stop button on his smartphone.

'There's a lot more. Enough for us to convince any jury to put the culprits away for a long stint at Her Majesty's pleasure. Justice will be served. We recovered the urine sample from Joe Sharkey's house. Sure enough, it tested positive for Ricin. On the recordings we also found proof that Mayor Ferguson and Mickey Cavandish sold a lot of freeholds to Sharkey at a much lower-than-market price over many years. It's all there. We've got them.'

McCartney then took a long breath and said, 'None of this would have happened without the work of three people. Jane Wilson, Sanjay Singh, and Steve Whittley. To Jane, I am pleased to give her this special medal of merit, the Queen's Police Medal, for her amazing devotion to duty. For Sanjay Singh I promise you will always be the first to be informed of the crime stories that come out of this building. For Steve Whittley, if you'll just excuse me for a few short minutes, I will now go back to my office to get his warrant card to officially reinstate him.'

At this point Jane, Steve and Sanjay, who were standing proudly at the front of the group, looked at each other in panic. Steve's warrant card? Jane had never put it back into the safe. It was still with Steve. Shit!

Steve grabbed the card from his trouser pocket and quickly handed it to Jane, who excused herself from the meeting, saying she urgently needed the toilet.

Sanjay took the floor. 'Sir, may I sincerely thank you on behalf of the *Liverpool Post* and all the people of this great city. You have truly done a wonderful job and the force is going to miss you when you retire.'

'Well, Mr. Singh, it's funny you should mention that. My plans have changed. I had a call from London earlier this morning. Due to the resounding success of Operation Croft the central government, who have taken temporary control of our city council, gently asked me to delay my retirement by two years. How could I possibly refuse? When needed, I'm there. Always have been, always will be. Of course, my wife is not too happy and our cottage in Wales will have to wait. However, she accepts that dedication to duty has always been at the forefront of all that I do, as it is for all of us gathered here today to celebrate a victory for justice. Now let me fetch that warrant for DI Whittley.'

'Just one further question DCI McCartney,' interjected Sanjay, seeing that Jane had not yet returned. 'What will happen to the Sharkey Group?'

'The recordings implicate Joe Sharkey, so he can no longer be the Chairman of the company and will go to prison, as will the Mayor, Mickey Cavandish and Andy Backland. The liquidators of the Sharkey

Group have decided to reimburse the four-thousand leaseholders the forty million they were owed. And the company will now go up for auction. As for Vanessa Chan, who is also clearly implicated in Lania's testimonial, we issued an arrest warrant. However, we received notice from Customs and Excise yesterday that she took a plane out of the country on Sunday morning, destination Beijing.'

Sixty-Five

Saturday evening, April 24, 2021, Beijing, China

Benny Zhang, his niece Vanessa Chan, and Jenny Wang – at least that was still her name for the moment - were seated at the best table at the *1949 Hidden City* restaurant in the Chaoyang district of Beijing. Outside the entrance, a giant, somewhat unflattering sculpture of Chairman Mao surveyed everyone coming and going into one of the city's top eateries.

Zhang loved this place. It had become a second home to him.

'Sometimes we win, and sometimes we learn, don't we ladies? We're playing the long game and Sharkey gave us a lot of food for thought. Time to move on now. I'm told that there are some interesting development opportunities in another small northern city in England. What's it called again Vanessa?'

'Newcastle,' she replied enthusiastically. 'The local folk call themselves Geordies.'

'That's the one. A former shipbuilding city for the British empire if I'm not mistaken. The ancestors of those Geordies probably built the gunboats that sailed up the Hai River to bomb the city of Tianjin, where my great grandfather lived at the time in the eighteen fifties.'

'Exactly. Then the next year the British and French forces stormed the old summer palace in Beijing. What an unrepeatable humiliation for our now great nation! And they think we're the aggressive ones? Such hypocrisy. I hate them,' Vanessa said, getting redder in the face as she spoke.

'Calm down my dear niece. Anger will get you nowhere. I'm going to name our Newcastle project Operation Gunboat Revenge. This time we need to learn from our mistakes. Had Sharkey not made those recordings and left them in that bank vault, we'd have made it good. Such is life. We've got time, haven't we?'

Zhang relaxed into his king-like seat at his favourite hang-out and reflected for a moment.

'Now what's a good wine to go with our Peking duck today? Why not our very own Silver Heights Family Reserve from Ningxia? I bought that winery fifteen years ago. You never know, it may turn out to be the best investment I'll ever make. Nothing like a bit of home-grown goodness. *Bon appetit!*'